THE DETENTION CLUB

DAVID YOO

Balzer + Bray
An Imprint of HarperCollins*Publishers*

Balzer + Bray is an imprint of HarperCollins Publishers.

The Detention Club
Copyright © 2011 by David Yoo

Library of Congress Cataloging-in-Publication Data
Yoo, David, date.
The detention club / by David Yoo. — 1st ed.
   p. cm.
   Summary: Sixth-grader Peter Lee, in a desperate attempt to regain the popularity he
had in elementary school, discovers that serving detention can win him important
friends, much to the dismay of his over-achieving eighth-grade sister, Sunny.
   ISBN 978-0-06-178378-4 (trade bdg. : alk. paper)
   [1. Middle schools—Fiction. 2. Schools—Fiction. 3. Brothers and sisters—Fiction.
4. Popularity—Fiction. 5. Conduct of life—Fiction. 6. Korean Americans—Fiction.]
I. Title.
PZ7.Y8155Det 2011   2010046211
[Fic]—dc22   CIP
                                                                                    AC

Typography by Jennifer Rozbruch
11 12 13 14 15   LP/RRDH   10 9 8 7 6 5 4 3 2
❖
First Edition

For Griffin Young Yoo

one

WHY IS IT THAT WHENEVER KIDS do something wrong, their parents always tell them to think about what they did? As if the only reason (*insert bad thing*) happened was because the kid simply didn't stop to consider the consequences before doing it. I guess it makes sense if your kid's under the age of three, tops. Say a toddler, for instance, sees an outlet in the wall and immediately sticks a metal fork in it—in that scenario I can see how his parents would wrongly assume that the kid wasn't thinking when he did that. But the truth is, even at age three, the little kid knows *exactly* what he's doing when he sticks the fork in the outlet. I know this for a fact because ol' Electro Boy was me, and I remember that I had a decent reason for doing it, too (I was trying to make my fork come to life).

In my own parents' defense, all semester I've kinda helped them believe that I don't think whenever I do something stupid, because anytime they ask me why I did something that upset them, I always answer, "I don't know." We just got through another one of those Q&A sessions a minute ago. They really put me through the wringer this time, asking me questions about everything that happened this semester, and each time I just kinda looked up at them dumbly and repeated the same answer. Here's a sampling of our deep conversation:

Mom: Why did you steal the poisonous chemicals from science class?
Me: I don't know.
Dad: What about the talent show—why would you put your life in danger like that?
Me: I don't know.
Mom: Why can't you get your act together with your schoolwork?
Me: I don't know.
Dad: Well then, how did Drew sprain his ankle?
Me: I don't know.
Mom: Why did your sister—
Me: I don't know.
Dad: At least tell us why you started that fire on

school grounds?

ME: I don't know.

Here's a secret: I know the answer to *all* of these questions, but I had no choice but to play dumb. I know my parents, and the truth would just make them more mad or sad or confused, so I just play dumb in order to spare them the additional heartache. In that sense, it's nice of me that I always pretend not to know why I do these things, isn't it? It makes me look like an idiot, which technically makes me a martyr.

My parents tried every trick in the book to get me to answer their questions. They threatened that they're going to have to send me to military school if I don't shape up. Actually, the threat wasn't even a trick—I might not have a choice, the way things are going. They got so desperate, they even promised me at one point to take me out for ice cream if I just answered their questions. That was their best move, and I almost broke down because I'm really in the mood for ice cream right now. It would help wash out the flavor of my mom's ninetieth horrible dinner in a row (I keep track), but I didn't budge. Finally my dad shook his head and said what he always says in the end when they finally give up:

"Young man, I want you to sit here and think about what you did."

He glared at me one last time before following my mom out of the room, shutting the door behind them. Then they marched straight into my sister Sunny's bedroom next door and tried squeezing some answers out of her.

I gasped for air—apparently I'd been holding my breath this whole time. I crept over to the wall between our bedrooms and cupped my right ear against it. My parents' low voices were muffled, but I could make out Sunny chirping, "I don't know," just like me, and despite everything that's happened this fall, I couldn't help but smile, because it was officially the first time in my sister's life that she didn't have an answer for everything.

two

I FIGURE THIS STORY BEGINS ON the last weekend of summer vacation, because that's when I received an important letter in the mail, so let's start right in at breakfast on Saturday. The big news in the Lee household that morning was that on Thursday, classes were going to begin, and I was going to be attending the same school as my sister for the first time since we moved here. Sunny was going to be an eighth grader at Fenwick Middle, while I'd be starting sixth. She hated that we were about to be going to school together. I knew this because I caught her glaring at me from across the table, and when I asked her what her problem was, she said, "I hate that we're going to school together."

"Why's that, honey?" Mom asked.

"Because he's an utter moron," Sunny replied.

5

"Why don't you tell me how you really feel?" I said.

"Peter Lee, quit being smart," Mom said.

My mom tends to favor my sister, and it shows in moments like this.

"I'm confused," I said, repeatedly pinching my chin and then pulling my hand out and looking at it, as if I have a really long beard (it makes me feel older when I do this). "Surely I can't be both, so which is it? Am I smart, or am I a moron?"

My mom's face changed from annoyed to concerned.

"Oh, sweetie, you're not a moron," she said soothingly.

"I wasn't actually confused," I muttered.

"Sounds like mom thinks you're a moron, too," Sunny said, smirking at me.

On this point I had to agree with her. I touched my pancakes to see if they were cool enough to squeeze into doughy balls, but they were still too hot. I always smush them into balls because they taste better that way. I do this with pretty much all bread products.

"Nobody in this family's a moron. Look at this, I even have proof!" my dad announced as he entered the kitchen. He handed me an already opened letter. "Son, you've just received some wonderful news from the school. Go on, share it with everyone."

"Ahem," I said, then coughed a couple of times, because

that's what people seem to do right before they start reading something out loud in front of a big group. And then I began reading:

Dear Peter,

I'm pleased to inform you that you have been preselected by your elementary-school teachers for inclusion in The Academically Gifted (T.A.G.) program here at Fenwick Middle School, which meets after school every other Wednesday.

This year the theme of our program is inventions. We'll be brainstorming and developing inventions that can change our world for the better! In late fall, at the Fenwick Middle School Inventors' Fair, we will select the most promising project from a young inventor to represent our school at the National Young Inventors' Competition, held in the spring in Washington, DC. This letter is to give you a chance for a head start.

Your objective is to start writing down ideas in an inventions notebook. We will focus on two types of inventions: fun/entertainment inventions, and environmental/eco-friendly inventions.

Good luck brainstorming, and I look forward to personally meeting you in the fall. Our first class is the third Wednesday in September—I can't wait!

Sincerely,

Claire Schoonmaker, MSW

Guidance Counselor

"I can't believe they chose you," Sunny said the second I finished reading. "Must be a weak incoming class."

"Sounds like you're jealous," I said.

Sunny laughed. It was her way of dealing with pain.

"You don't actually think you're smarter than me, do you?" she asked.

"I aced all my classes last year, too, and I didn't have to study all the time like you had to," I pointed out, and her face turned red because she knew it was true.

"You were in elementary school—that's not even real school! You got good grades for being able to write in cursive and color between the lines and stuff."

"And I didn't have to stay up late at night practicing coloring between the lines, did I?" I replied.

"Stop arguing," Dad snapped. "For once, I'd like to eat breakfast without the two of you going at it."

I turned my chair to face him so we could have a little one-on-one.

"So what do you know about this Schoonmaker lady?" I asked him.

"Sunny, would you please explain to your brother what the T.A.G. program is?"

"You're in the program, too?" I groaned.

"Of course I am. It's *supposed* to be a club for the smartest kids in school, although it sounds like they're changing the prerequisites," she said. "Last year we discussed current events and then competed in the Middle School Academic Bowl in the spring."

I'd forgotten about the Academic Bowl, because it was just one of a zillion activities Sunny participated in last year. Believe me, it's hard to keep track.

I felt bummed that Sunny was already in the program, but at the same time the fact that she was in it kinda made me feel that getting selected was that much more impressive, since she's basically considered the smartest student in the history of Fenwick. I looked at the letter again and got the chills—here was written proof that I was considered one of the smartest kids in school!

"I always knew you were special," Dad said, patting me on the shoulder.

"Maybe he should be put in special ed, then," Sunny said.

"He doesn't mean that kind of special," Mom said, quickly adding, "although there's nothing wrong with that."

I resumed smushing my rubbery pancake into a ball before eating it.

"Don't play with your food," she said.

"But you know this is how I like it. We've gone over this before, Mom. Sheesh."

"Maybe he's just invented a new kind of pancake," Dad suggested.

"You're right!" I held up the rubbery ball and stared at it. "All this time I had no idea I was sitting on a gold mine eating them this way. This thing's going to be worth millions."

"My son, the inventor!" said Dad, but when I offered to make him one, he immediately shielded his plate from me and muttered, "Ugh, no."

Sunny grimaced as I chewed on my pancake ball.

"There's nothing wrong with eating pancakes the boring old way like everyone else," I told her. "I'm sure you'll come up with some fine inventions on your own. Food's just not your thing, maybe."

"Maybe they'll start a caveman club for you to join," she suggested.

"Not to sound cocky, Dad," I said, ignoring her. "But I have to admit, I've always kinda known deep down that I was really special."

"I think I'm going to be sick," Sunny said.

"If you don't have anything positive to say to your brother, you can be excused," Dad said, cutting up his pancakes that old boring way.

"Fine, I'm out of here." Sunny pushed her chair back. "All I'll say, Peter, is that you're going to be in for a rude awakening on Thursday."

"Maybe this afternoon I'll help you work on your inventions," I called out after her. "It's no problem, really!"

Her bedroom door shut upstairs a couple of seconds later.

"I don't like that woman," I added, but my parents didn't nod in agreement like I wanted them to. Instead my dad sighed and put a hand on my shoulder.

"Blood's thicker than water, Peter, you know that," he said.

That was another one of his sayings. Dad always said it whenever Sunny and I fought. What he didn't realize was that the only thing my sister and I had in common was that we were related by blood—otherwise we couldn't be more different. The only other thing we had in common, I suppose, was that neither of us could stand the other. But of course that's not what my dad meant by giving me the ol' "blood is thicker than water" line. It's supposed to mean that since we're related we should be able to get past our differences, but I figured maybe the person who made up the saying meant it just technically, in which case I admit it's true. Blood *is* thicker than water. Woopity doo. So's orange juice.

Mom turned to me.

"Your sister's just—"

"Jealous," I finished her sentence for her. "I know."

"Actually, I was going to say she's stressed about school starting," she said.

three

I WENT UP TO MY BEDROOM after breakfast to start brainstorming inventions. I had a couple unused notebooks from elementary school (they were unused because I was the second-smartest student in my grade and so I didn't need them) and I picked out one to be my official inventions notebook. The smartest kid, in case you're curious, was Carson Santiago, aka the Human Calculator—that's his nickname because he's good at math and always lugs around this huge scientific calculator everywhere he goes. I've always tried to correct everyone by telling them that, technically, his nickname should actually be "The Human Who Owns a Calculator," but you just can't change nicknames once they're established, even if they're incredibly inaccurate.

I took out a pen and wrote THE INVENTIONS NOTEBOOK on the front of it in big blocky letters and then turned to the first page. No ideas magically entered my brain, so I reread Ms. Schoonmaker's letter. We were supposed to come up with two types of inventions—environmental and fun inventions. I thought, what's the most enjoyable, fun thing in the world? The answer was obvious.

Cats.

And what was it everyone loves so much about cats? That they're little, and soft. So how could I improve on the current form of household cat? The answer came to me the moment I thought up the question, and it made me feel dizzy with excitement.

Make them *smaller.*

I then spent a couple of minutes drawing really tiny cats the size of a coffee mug. Then I drew coffee mugs next to them to prove how tiny they were. But that's when reality set in. How could I possibly make cats smaller? It was pretty obvious that, as smart as I was, this idea was way out of my league, but then a couple of seconds later I realized that there *was* a way. My dad always says that sometimes it's hard to see things that are too obvious. One time, to get me and my best friend, Drew, to stop playing video games all day, he hid a broken bike reflector in the backyard and had us look for it, and we searched for over an hour before giving up and heading back in to play more video games. The point, however, was that it turned out my dad had simply put the reflector right on the railing of the deck in plain sight.

I needed a cat to test out the idea, though, and unfortunately my dad's allergic, so we're not allowed to own any. Drew, however, has one, so I picked up the phone and started dialing.

"Newmark residence," Drew said.

"It's me. I have a question for you, but before I ask it, I have another question—can you keep an open mind when I ask you my main question in a couple of seconds?"

"I guess."

"Okay, then," I said, and took a deep breath. "How would you feel if—and there's no guarantee this would actually happen—Fluffy died during an experiment that had the chance to make the world a better place for everyone?"

Drew gasped into the receiver.

"That would crush me!" Drew said, then I heard him put the phone down and shout, "Fluffy? Where are you?"

"I was afraid you were going to say that," I muttered. "Well, what if I signed a written contract that said if your cat died during some experiments, I'd totally buy you a new, even better cat, would that make you happy?"

"Pete, you're scaring me," he said. "What the heck are you talking about?"

14

Sunny's bedroom door opened, and I whispered into the receiver, "I can't say right now. I'll come over."

"Why can't you just tell me now?"

"Because these walls have ears!" I shouted, but then I heard her talking to Mom downstairs.

"Well, today's Counting Day, anyway," Drew said.

Drew was right! We'd been going crazy all summer waiting for Counting Day to come, and I guess I got so excited about the letter that morning that I forgot all about it.

"I'll see you in ten minutes," I said, and hung up.

I rolled up the notebook and wedged it into my back pocket, then headed downstairs. Sunny was in the living room with my mom, practicing the flute. She'd been practicing a couple of hours every day all summer, when she wasn't studying for the SATs, which she's not even going to take for three more years. Mom's a nurse, and when she's home from work she usually sits there while Sunny practices, holding a metronome in her lap, which is this little box that keeps the beat (it's not much of an invention, really—basically it's a ticking clock that can't tell time) and nods along as Sunny plays the same stupid piece over and over.

"Where are you going?" Mom asked.

"I'm going to work on some inventions over at Drew's house," I said.

Sunny kept playing, but I could tell she was listening

because her eyebrows got all scrunched up, as if she was mad at her sheet music.

"That's great, sweetie!" Mom said. "You've already started a notebook?"

"You might as well book a flight down to DC in the spring so you can see me win the contest."

Sunny blew too hard into her flute and it made an awful squeak, and I made a big show by covering my ears. "I've known about the theme for this year's T.A.G. class since the spring," she said. "I have a whole notebook full of ideas already."

My stomach dropped.

"I'm sure your ideas are wonderful, Peter," Mom said.

Drew's house is a five-minute walk away, at the other end of Brook Street. We met on the bus ride home after the first day of fourth grade. I had gone over to Drew's house, and he had this huge box full of Matchbox cars on the shelf behind his desk. Even though he no longer played with them, he still collected them, and he was embarrassed when I saw them—but then I brought him over to my house and showed him my stamp collection, my marble collection, and my big bag full of twist ties that I collect every week after my mom gets groceries. I couldn't care less about stamps, and I don't even know how to play with marbles—Sunny just had a bunch of them that she lost interest in and I inherited the collection.

It turned out we're both really into collecting things, and in school this was a huge advantage. For two straight years our class won the Campbell's Soups label contest, which is this annual event to raise money for the homeless. The reason our class won was because me and Drew worked together like an assembly line, steaming the labels off of every can in our kitchen pantries in order for the labels to come off perfectly, with no rips. This annoyed my parents because they had to deal with months of Russian-roulette dinners since they had no idea what was in any of the now unlabeled cans.

"Okay, looks like we're having balsamic chicken and"— Mom would open a tin can and sigh—"pumpkin-pie filling for dinner."

"I hate you, Son," Dad would say.

Every day at recess Drew and I would go about collecting something, anything, just to be the best at it. By the end of recess everyone was obsessed with trying to collect it, too. One day it would be those white pebbles over by the tire swings. Another day it would be strips of bark off the dogwood trees lining the main entrance (the principal wasn't thrilled with that one). Drew and I collected a pile of acorns one recess that would have made any squirrel jealous.

For two years that's the main thing me and Drew did

when we hung out—we collected stuff. And for the entire summer before sixth grade we'd been collecting just one thing: mica. Mica is that shiny, glasslike flaky stuff that you can find on boulders in the woods. It's really brittle and cool to look at, and once I peeled off my first piece, I knew I had to have more. Drew did, too. Back in the spring me and Drew realized that all the boulders behind his house are covered with the stuff, so we started collecting it, and we brought some pieces on the last day of school to show our classmates, and everyone agreed to have a contest to see who could collect the most over the summer. Drew and I made a vow to not count the collection until the end of the summer so it would be a huge surprise to us when we finally tallied the numbers.

I made the final turn onto the stretch of Brook Street with Drew's house on it. He was waiting for me out on his front stoop, and waved when he saw me.

"What's in your back pocket?" he asked.

"Which pocket?" I asked, as if I didn't know there was a gigantic notebook sticking out of it.

He rolled his eyes.

"Your back right pocket."

"Why, that would be my right butt cheek," I said, and we both laughed.

"Did you just make that up?" he asked.

"Yup! Now ask me what's in my left back pocket," I said.

"But I already know the answer, Pete."

"No, you don't," I said, but Drew didn't believe me. "Come on, just ask me."

"Fine, what's in your left back pocket?"

"Some lint."

Drew looked at me.

"That's not funny," he said.

"Oh, and my left butt cheek!" I shouted, and we howled like insane wolves.

"You should write that one down in your notebook," he said.

I took it out and patted the cover a couple of times. "No, I can't. This is a *special* notebook."

"What's it for?"

"My secret inventions," I said, and Drew's eyes widened.

"Does this have to do with killing my cat?" he whispered.

I nodded really seriously.

"I thought so," Drew said, looking behind him at the big bay window. "My mom might be listening. Let's continue this conversation in privacy, up at Corbett Canyon."

That's one other thing Drew and I have in common: We're both incredibly suspicious of other people, usually for no good reason.

four

CORBETT CANYON IS WHAT WE CALL the tree house in the back of Drew's house. It's the name that was on one of the bottles of wine my parents received at their holiday party last winter, and I just liked the classy sound of it. The tree house isn't a traditional tree house, but an old storage shed that used to be in Drew's backyard. When his parents got divorced, his dad, before moving out, got a couple of his air-force buddies to help him hoist the storage shed up into a tree because he'd always promised to build his son a tree house. It worked out well that he never got around to it, because I doubt any tree house he made would have been as nice as the storage shed; it's got a roof with shingles and everything. We keep two beach chairs in it and a metal safe that we store important stuff in. The only bad part about it is that before it became a tree house, it was where Mr. Newmark stored his lawn mower, so there's a permanent smell of gasoline that's seeped into the wood over the years, but your nose gets used to the stench after you hang out in it for a couple of minutes.

I explained the letter to Drew.

"So what's the big invention?" he asked.

I explained my mini cats idea.

"My favorite time with Fluffy was when she was a kitten," Drew admitted.

"See? All cat owners probably say that. And isn't it a shame you can't always have your cat in the size you enjoy her the most?

"Oh, okay, I'm seeing it! God, you're smart."

"You'd think it would get old hearing people say that all the time, but I have to say, not really."

"But how would you make Fluffy smaller?"

"Easy. All we have to do is this simple procedure—I hate to even call it that, really—where we make a tiny incision into Fluffy's back and take out most of her spinal cord."

Drew stared at me for a couple of seconds.

"That's your idea?" he finally said.

At first I felt mad that this noninventor would even think to question my idea, but then I reminded myself that not all of us have vision.

"Think about it—the spinal cord is the reason why cats are as big as they are."

"I'm not sure that would work, though."

"Well, being an inventor's all about taking risks."

"But she's my cat, so *you're* not taking a risk."

"But I am, I really like Fluffy," I said, but this didn't convince him so I added, "and I'm willing to risk our relationship, too, that's how confident I am this idea works."

"I'd never allow it, but it doesn't even matter, you wouldn't be able to perform the surgery. You hate the sight of blood, remember?"

"Only my own," I sniffed.

"Honestly, do you really think you could take a scalpel to a cat?"

I thought about it for a minute.

"I was kinda hoping you'd be up for the job, buddy," I finally said. "Otherwise I won't be able to share the patent with you."

"There has to be another way."

I sighed.

"Honestly, Drew, I'd be lying if I said I wasn't a little disappointed in you."

Nothing I said could guilt him into agreeing to operate on his own cat, though, so we just sat there for a few minutes, trying to think of less gory ways to shrink cats, but nothing came to us. It didn't matter—just sitting right next to our collection of mica made us both want to get on with the official count, so we switched gears and proceeded with Counting Day. Drew took out his clipboard and pen, and I opened up the safe and carefully pulled out the old green canvas bag his dad let him have a long time ago.

"Are you scared about going to Fenwick Middle?" Drew asked as we started carefully taking out the pieces and lining them up in rows of ten.

"Why would I be scared?" I asked. "Drew, look at all this mica around us. We had half this number of pieces at the beginning of summer. We're the best collectors in our grade, remember?"

"But half the kids are from Hemenway Elementary across town, and we don't know any of them. And there's going to be all those older kids. Remember those guys who chased us on their bikes at the beginning of summer?"

"Relax. Once we win the mica contest, it'll make us the new kings of the middle school, and everyone from Hemenway will worship us, and then on top of that, with me in T.A.G., we'll be liked by everyone else in no time."

"Plus, your sister's the queen of the school, so that should help," he added.

"Sunny and I hate each other, remember?" I said.

"Well, it never hurts to be related to the queen of the school."

"You're probably right," I admitted. "But it doesn't matter. Middle school's going to be exactly like elementary school. It's just a different building, and there will be some older kids. No big deal."

We finished laying out the lines of mica pieces and Drew started counting them, doing the math on his clipboard. I rocked back and forth on my knees, waiting for the final tally. When he was done, he put down the clipboard and pretended to frown.

"Hit me with it," I said.

"It's official," Drew shouted. "We're the greatest collectors of mica in the history of mankind! We have two hundred forty pieces!"

We both fell back onto our backs and just laughed our heads off for a couple of minutes. Apparently, getting really shocking news makes you do that.

"Life can't get much better than this," Drew finally said, sitting back up.

"You can say that again."

"Life can't get much better than this."

I frowned at him.

"I didn't actually mean to say it again."

"I know, but it felt so good to say it the first time," he replied.

"Hey, whatever makes you happy," I said, patting my best pal on the back.

five

SUNNY HITCHED A RIDE WITH Dad on the first day of school, because she had morning band practice. She's the best flute player in the band because nobody else willingly spends their entire summers practicing their band instrument nonstop. My parents wanted me to join band, too, but I flat-out refused, simply because there was no way I was going to wake up extra early every morning.

My parents used to make us both give music recitals during their dinner parties. I learned to play the recorder in second grade, and whenever we had company over, Sunny would give a performance after dinner, and then my parents would make me play the recorder. After a few dinner parties my parents stopped asking me to play, because Sunny was playing these really hard classical pieces and it just made me look stupid. Later Drew and I turned my recorder into a sweet fireworks launcher—the holes in the recorder are the perfect size for bottle rockets. Drew's dad secretly gives him fireworks whenever he visits, so he asked for a recorder last Christmas—that way we could really battle it out in the woods behind his house.

Drew lives a couple of blocks away from Fenwick Middle School, so we'd be walking directly from his house every day. This was good news, because I'd always hated riding the bus back in elementary school. It smelled like exhaust fumes and there weren't any seat belts. I've never understood that about adults. They yell at us all the time about wearing our seat belts, but they think nothing of us riding twice a day in a big yellow bus that doesn't even have armrests, let alone seat belts. It's weird, because I hate wearing my seat belt when I ride in cars, but on buses you'll find me pressing my knees against the seat in front of me to make me feel more secure in case we get T-boned by a semi.

It was chilly out as I walked over to Drew's house, but I'd forced myself to wear a T-shirt and no jacket because I used to overdress back in elementary school. By lunchtime I'd be sweating like crazy, even in the middle of winter, and on top of that I lost three winter jackets in fifth grade alone. I hadn't figured it would be this cold out in the mornings, though.

"I can see you shivering from here," Drew said when I showed up. "Why aren't you wearing a jacket?"

"I don't want to talk about it," I snapped. "And it's rude to stare at someone when they're in this much physical pain."

"Do you want to borrow my jacket?" he suggested.

"Sure! Thanks," I said, whipping off my backpack. I zipped up his jacket, and a couple of seconds later I felt nice and toasty. Now Drew was the one shivering. "You look really cold."

"Can I have my jacket back?"

I glared at him.

"You're not going to grow up to be one of those adults who give homeless people a dollar and then a second later ask for it back because you suddenly want a soda or something?"

"What adult does that?"

"Plenty, and the homeless hate their guts."

"Fine, keep the stupid jacket," he said, rubbing his hands together.

"I heard that stomping your feet warms you up," I suggested.

He started stomping his feet as we walked to school.

"It's working! Thanks for the tip."

"Don't mention it."

A minute later we were staring at the main entrance

to the school. I suddenly felt a pile of dead frogs in my stomach as I pictured a lobby full of older kids. I turned to Drew. He looked like he had dead frogs in his stomach, too.

"Are you nervous?" I asked.

"No, I'm just really cold."

I glared at him.

"You know it makes me feel bad when you keep saying things like that."

"I'm sorry," he said. Drew can be pretty insensitive sometimes, but his heart's in the right place, so I try not to judge him for it. "So are you scared about going in there?"

"Who said anyone was scared?" I said.

Drew just looked at me with unblinking eyes. It's a fact that best friends can talk with their eyes. And his eyes were telling me two things:

Peter, I totally understand, and

Peter, I really want my jacket back.

"Come on, let's head inside," I said quickly so he wouldn't ask for his jacket back again, and he followed me up to the double doors.

The lobby was full of students, and I was shocked at how big everyone looked. Not just the older kids—everyone from our grade seemed bigger, too! Apparently Drew and I missed a summer field trip to a cornfield where a pulsing meteor landed or something, because everyone in our grade, even the girls, had grown a lot over the summer. I counted five boys in my grade with beginner mustaches (and two girls, for that matter).

"Who should we tell first about our mica collection?" Drew asked me.

"Don't tell anyone just yet," I said. "Play it cool, let's get a feel for how much mica everyone else collected over the summer, just in case someone collected more. Then we can sneak home during recess and collect more."

"Do you think somebody actually beat us?"

"Of course not, but it would be foolish not to allow for the possibility."

"You have a point." Drew admitted. "There's Trent."

Trent and his basketball buddies, Lance and Paul, were standing by the fire exit. Back in elementary school Trent and his buddies were considered kinda weird, because every day at recess instead of playing kickball with all of us normal people they shot hoops by themselves the entire time. Trent looked like he'd grown a foot. They were standing with two other guys I didn't recognize.

We walked over to them.

"You grew a lot this summer," I said to Trent.

"It's called puberty," Trent said. "You guys should try it sometime."

"But seriously, you must be the biggest kid in school already."

For some reason Trent didn't take this as a compliment and laughed at me.

"This is Kyle and Mark, they went to Hemenway," Trent said. "We played on the same rec league hoops team this summer."

"And for your information, *those* are the biggest kids in school," Lance said, pointing over at two identical twins in the corner. They looked like adult mechanics or something, and I couldn't help but turn away when they glanced in our direction. "And you shouldn't go near them."

"Who are they?" Drew asked.

"Only the two biggest bullies in the school! Meet Hank and Hugh Sweet, aka the Sweet brothers," Kyle said. "I heard the school board over the summer tried to make it official that the brothers held the world record for most detentions in a row, but the *Guinness Book of World Records* rejected the claim because they didn't want to reward criminals."

"Dude, that's crazy," I said, gaping at Drew.

"Note-to-self . . . must-not . . . ever-get . . . detention," Drew said in a funny robot voice, and I giggled.

"Yeah, no kidding, and I'll pretend you didn't just talk in a stupid robot voice," Lance replied, and I casually changed my giggling to coughing. He added, "Anyway—they were the biggest bullies in school last year, too."

"So what'd you guys do all summer?" Trent asked Drew.

"Funny you should ask—," he started saying with a big smile on his face, but I cut him off.

"Nothing, really," I said, glaring at Drew. "So Trent, did you do anything else besides play hoops like a weirdo all summer? Did you spend any time in, say, the woods?"

"Huh?" Trent said, and his new Hemenway pals just stared at me as if I'd just asked the dumbest question ever.

The bell rang, and everyone started heading upstairs to the classrooms.

"Jackpot," I whispered to Drew, and he stared at me funny, too.

"Why would Trent spend any time in the woods? What's in the woods?"

"Don't you get it?" I said. "He totally forgot about the mica contest because he was too busy playing basketball all summer! And he's our main competition. This is turning out better than I expected."

"That is good news!"

"Oh, and one more thing," I added. "Don't ever use that robot voice again with those guys, you're embarrassing both of us."

"Sorry." Drew blushed. "You should've told me it wasn't

the right moment to bust it out."

"I assumed you knew," I said, not looking at him.

Drew and I had homeroom together because our last names are close together. The school is set up like this: The lobby and gym and teachers' lounge are out front, facing the parking lot on one side and a soccer field on the other. The academic wing of the school is behind this section—it's two floors, and completely circular, with the classrooms on the outside. On the inside of the second floor is the library, and on the first floor the middle is the cafeteria and auditorium. We got to room 27 and our homeroom teacher, Mr. Davis, handed us our class schedules. We compared them and discovered that we didn't have any classes together! I groaned. This was bad news, I'd never had a class without Drew in it up to this point. It was kinda like we were teammates in class back in elementary school.

"At least we have homeroom and lunch together," Drew said.

We grabbed some seats near the back.

The Human Calculator and his brainiac pals were sitting in a cluster behind us.

"How-was-your-sum-mer?" I asked him in a robot voice, winking at Drew so he could see that this was one of those situations where a robot voice made perfect sense. I talk like that to Carson to secretly make fun of him being such a nerd. He never gets it—which means he's not nearly as smart as everyone thinks.

"I visited my grandparents in Mexico City for most of it," he said.

"What kind of rock formations do they have in Mexico City?" I asked.

"Why would you care, are you a geologist or something?"

"Just curious, and for the record, yes, I probably am a geolowhatever-you-just-called me," I said, winking at Drew. It seemed like everyone had forgotten about the mica contest! We'd win just by default, which was fine by me.

Sally Leathers was also in our homeroom. In fourth grade, all the girls worshipped Sally because she was really fast—during one recess she actually beat Trent and some other guys in a race, but then in fifth grade she gave up her running career to focus on riding horses, and as a result her legs weakened and she fell to third-fastest girl in the grade, and people just weren't as crazy about her as before. She looked different, I noticed. Not just taller, but she was wearing makeup and looked older than us.

"What'd you do this summer?" I asked Sally. "I mean, besides age ten years."

"It was boring. I hung out at the pool every day, but I met my new BFF, Angie. She went to Hemenway," Sally said,

34

pointing at the girl next to her.

"Hi," I said to Angie, and she kinda just stared back at me.

"What about you guys?" Sally asked.

Drew looked at me. I figured Trent and his basketball buds spent the entire summer playing hoops, and Carson spent his time in Mexico City, and it sounded like everyone else hung out at the pool, so I assumed we'd definitely collected the most mica. Everyone was paying attention to us, so I figured it was a good time to make the official announcement. I nodded at him.

"Pete and I more than doubled our mica collection," he said.

At first nobody said anything.

"You guys collect mica?" Angie asked.

"That's what we do at our school," I reminded her. "I guess you don't have any on your side of the town. Drew and I had the most at the end of the year, but we barely had thirty pieces, remember, Sally?"

"Nobody plays with mica anymore, Pete!" Carson snickered. "That is *so* fifth grade."

Everyone laughed.

"We don't play with it," Drew shouted. "Mica's not a toy. If you knew anything about it, you'd know that you have to be really careful with it, and besides, you don't—"

Thankfully, the bell rang for first period, so Drew couldn't continue doing what he mistakenly thought was effective damage control. Everyone raced out of the room, including Drew, while I sat back in my seat, thinking about what Carson had said. "*So* fifth grade"? What was that supposed to mean?

Six

IN ADDITION TO FINDING OUT I didn't have any classes with Drew and then discovering that nobody seemed to remember the mica contest, I found out that all the teachers were in love with Sunny. I mean, I'd already assumed this, but it weirded me out that in all my classes that morning, the teachers introduced themselves to me and raved about how great Sunny was.

"Any relation to Sunny Lee?" Mrs. Ryder, my first-period math teacher, asked.

"That's my sister," I said.

"Sunny was my brightest student last year," she said, then added, "I expect big things from you this year, Peter."

I didn't say anything.

"Peter may be smartest," Sally said. "But he still plays with mica!"

Everyone laughed.

"I'm not sure you're in a position to tease me like that—let's not forget that last we checked, you were only the third-fastest girl in the grade," I pointed out.

Sally stared at me.

"What are you talking about?" she said.

Mr. Vensel, my English teacher, and even Mrs. Lewis, my art teacher, both noted my relationship to Sunny. Then they'd start talking about the class, and kids would pull out their notebooks and take notes. I didn't feel like I had to do this because I've always been ahead in class, so instead I stared out the windows all morning, thinking of things Drew and I could collect outside during recess. That was the key, I figured. Everyone had forgotten about mica, so we just had to remind everyone how good we were at collecting stuff in general.

I realized we couldn't just collect something we'd already collected back in elementary school. It would have to be something different. I stared out the windows and wondered, what's different outside that they don't have at Fenwick Elementary? But the grass and trees all looked the same. Where the heck was the playground, for that matter?

Drew was already waiting for me at an empty table when I got to the caf for lunch. He waved at me, and I nodded over at the lunch lines. I did a double take. There were *two* lines for lunch? Back in elementary school there was only one line, and we all got served the same thing. In middle school I discovered that there was now a line for "hot lunch" and another for "à la carte." I had no clue what "à la carte" meant, but I saw that they were serving plastic lasagna for hot lunch, so I got in line behind Carson and tapped him on the shoulder.

"You speak Spanish. What does 'à la carte' mean?" I asked him.

He grimaced at me.

"It's French, for one thing," he snapped. "And it just means you pick and choose what you want to eat. But you won't be able to buy anything—they only accept cash, not mica."

Why was Carson talking so tough with me? Just a few months earlier, in fifth grade, he'd almost been too shy to even approach me, and sometimes I'd catch him just staring at me fondly from a distance after I'd done something really impressive, like juggle the blackboard erasers for ten seconds or catch an out in kickball during recess.

He turned away from me. I figured he was just still feeling nervous about being in this new place. I bought a lukewarm cheeseburger (apparently, a red lightbulb isn't a reliable heat source) and an apple juice and brought my tray back to Drew's table. "Why are you sitting alone?" I asked.

"I don't know," he said, as if he was noticing this for the first time. "Maybe everyone's talking about their classes or something."

"Did you know there was going to be an à la carte line?"

He shook his head.

"I don't like Spanish food anyway," he said.

"It's French," I corrected him.

"You're so wise," Drew said, and I didn't bother admitting that I'd just learned this little factoid myself, because the guy considered me a genius and I didn't want to let him down.

"So what are we going to do about the mica situation?" Drew asked. "We collected so much of it for nothing."

"The way I see it, okay, so mica may have gone out of style, but we just have to get everyone collecting stuff during recess and they'll remember how cool we were."

"Thank God you're good at thinking on your toes," Drew said.

I blushed.

"I'm no different from any other great inventor," I said humbly.

We sat there eating our lunches, watching everyone laugh and talk with kids from Hemenway as if they'd been best friends since birth. Lunch was divided by grade, and this was our first time seeing the entire sixth grade together at once. Sally and her horse-riding friends were sitting with a group of girls from Hemenway who probably rode horses, too. Carson and his brainiac pals were sitting with some new kids who looked really smart—one of them had easily the biggest head I've ever seen in my life. Trent and his basketball buddies were sitting with Kyle and Mark, the two kids we'd met before homeroom. The band kids were with Hemenway band kids, I could tell because they had their instrument cases on the ground next to them. Even the quietest people from our grade were sitting with new kids. It didn't look like they were talking much—they were probably the quietest kids from Hemenway, too. But the fact is they were sitting together, and looked like they'd been sitting together for years even though this was only the first day of school. The part that bugged me the most was that Drew and I were definitely the only ones sitting at an unfilled table.

After lunch everyone got let out into the main lobby of the school, where we stood in a big confused group, like cattle.

"Why aren't they letting us out for recess?" I whispered to Drew.

"Maybe they're waiting for someone to take the lead?" he suggested, and I got all excited.

"Follow me," I said, and we made our way through the

41

throng of students to the double doors. I pushed them open, and immediately a teacher shouted at me and charged over.

"Where do you think you're going?" she demanded.

Students looked over at us.

"Uh . . . recess?" I said.

Sally and Angie were standing near the doors at that moment.

"There's no recess in middle school!" Angie cried. She turned around and shouted, "Peter and Drew are trying to go outside for recess!"

Everyone laughed at us.

"Are you going to look for mica out there or something?" Sally asked.

We slunk over to an empty corner of the lobby and stood against the brick wall.

"No recess? How do they expect us to calm down after lunch?" Drew whispered.

"I have no idea," I admitted. "You'd think someone would have told us about this earlier."

In our defense, a lot of the sixth graders also seemed pretty confused about not having recess, but they pretended to be cool with it. Turns out the school didn't even have a playground anywhere on the premises, just a crummy soccer field outside of the teachers' lounge, used by the sports teams and gym classes. Instead of having recess, we were expected to just hang out in the front lobby after lunch for fifteen minutes, where we could "talk" like adults or something.

Aside from the short burst of laughter people had when we tried to go outside for recess, it was kinda quiet in the lobby that first day. The sixth graders stood around in groups, just looking at each other.

"Now what?" Drew asked.

"I guess we're going to have to improvise."

"What does that mean?"

"We're just going to have to find stuff to collect in our classrooms this afternoon."

"How do we know they'll like it? Maybe nobody collects stuff anymore."

"That's impossible," I said. "It's embedded in our DNA to want to collect stuff."

"What does that even mean?" he asked.

It's a phrase I learned from my dad during the summer when I threw a rock at the sliding glass door one day in plain sight of my parents, and shattered it.

My parents gasped.

"Why on earth would you do that?" Mom cried.

"Don't bother trying to understand him; it's embedded in his DNA," Dad said.

Anyway, because of this, I still figured collecting stuff

was the key to getting people to remember that they used to worship us.

"Kids in our grade are just making fun of us because the Hemenway kids weren't into collecting mica last year, so they don't want to look bad, but we just have to show them how cool we really are," I explained.

"But there's nothing to collect in class," Drew complained.

"Use your imagination. Trust me—I'm sure the class-rooms are full of stuff."

Drew had a point, though. Outside you were surrounded by all kinds of interesting stuff to collect, like clovers and twigs and broken glass, whereas the inside of a tiny class-room is slim pickings to begin with, never mind the fact that it gets cleaned every night by a janitor. At the start of social-studies class I searched the room for something to collect, but there wasn't anything good, and I had to settle. I made sure everyone was watching me (by coughing really loudly for a couple of seconds) before I started emptying out the pencil shavings in the pencil sharpener and stuffing the shavings down my pocket. It made my fingers all sooty, so I wiped the lead off on my white shirt.

"Why did you just wipe lead all over your shirt, Pete?" Lance asked me.

"I'm collecting pencil shavings," I said casually, pretending

I wasn't horrified that I'd just ruined my new shirt. "Everyone's doing it. Bet I can collect more than you!"

"But you collected all of it just now," he pointed out.

I looked at the empty sharpener.

"Oh—look at that," I said. "I guess that means I win!"

"Congratulations," he said, but he didn't look impressed in the slightest.

Drew didn't have any better luck. He tried getting everyone to collect hair from the floor in his social-studies class, and Donnie accused him of trying to make a wig. It was hopeless. By the time we got let out at the end of the day, I was feeling downright depressed. Everything we'd worked toward all summer had blown up in our faces.

Drew and I started our walk home. At the edge of the soccer field, before the big hill, we turned and watched all the buses pulling out of the parking lot in the front of the school. The buses' windows were all half-open, and you could hear everyone shouting and laughing as if it had been a really fun day. It suddenly dawned on me that we were no longer the kings of the school. This was Sunny's school, and we were just visitors.

"Are you okay?" Drew asked.

"We're in serious trouble," I said.

"What are you talking about?"

I put a hand on his shoulder, not so much to calm him

down but to steady myself, because I felt a little dizzy.

"I think we might be . . . losers," I admitted.

"That's impossible!" Drew laughed, but then he saw I was being serious. "Wait—you're kidding, right?"

Seven

I WASN'T. DREW TRAILED BEHIND ME as I marched all the way to Corbett Canyon. I opened the safe, took out the bag, and pulled out a handful of mica, shaking my head. How did I ever think this stuff was cool, I wondered? I started carelessly dropping the fragile pieces back into the bag.

"What do you think you're doing?" he asked. "Careful, Peter, you're going to break the biggest pieces."

I glared at him.

"Who cares?" I asked.

I zipped up the bag and stood up. Drew blocked the entrance.

"I demand to know what you plan on doing with that," he said.

"We're going to sell it in town so at least we make some dough for all our troubles," I said. "Now get out of my way."

"But you've always said it's only a matter of time before mica's worth millions, once all the miners in Pennsylvania run out of gold and silver, remember? You said we have to be patient, that it was our nest egg or whatever you called it, and—"

I made sure to talk real slowly so he'd understand.

"We've had a good system going, buddy, you don't want to mess it up," I said, but he wouldn't budge. "Look, you've always been really good at assuming I'm always right, that's how we work so well as friends, so I beg of you, and this is the last time I'm going to ask this, Drew: Step out of the way."

"No!"

"This," I said, holding up a piece of mica and waving it in front of his face, "is physical proof that we're pathetic. We're in middle school and we still collect mica?! What the heck were we thinking? Everyone was getting to know each other at the pool and playing basketball together while we were slaving away in the woods, peeling this junk off the boulders? It may be worth something, but what difference does it make if nobody in school thinks so?"

Drew held both hands out trying to calm me down.

"Peter, first of all, I'm not questioning how pathetic we

are, and second, PUT DOWN THE FRICKING MICA!"

He wasn't moving, and the only thing I could think to do was squeeze the mica in my hand and growl. The piece shattered immediately. I watched the tiny splinters fall to the wooden floor. "Please don't do this!" Drew screamed.

We rode our bikes over to the pawnshop in town. Drew tried the entire way to convince me to turn back, but I just pretended I couldn't hear him because of the wind. We went inside the store, I opened up the canvas bag for the creepy-looking owner, and he peered inside. The fluorescent light reflected off the precious metal inside and it made his cheeks light up.

"What's in there?" he asked.

"It's mica. Two hundred forty pieces," I said. "Well, I went over a speed bump pretty hard, so maybe it's closer to five hundred at this point. How much will you give us for it?"

The guy just stared at me for a little while.

"Kid, do you know why they call mica and pyrite fool's gold?" he finally said.

"Is that supposed to be funny?" I replied.

I tried to convince the guy to buy our mica stash, but he refused to believe that there was a market for it in the future. Drew was relieved. Eventually we pedaled back to the tree house. Drew took the bag from me because he could tell I was just going to let it drop onto the floor. He unzipped it and started gingerly taking out some pieces. He whimpered as he held up a jagged shard.

"I don't even recognize this piece," he cried. "You broke it!"

"You broke it!" I mimicked him, making my voice sound all weepy like Drew sounded when he said it, the big baby. "Now just give me the bag, Drew."

"No, leave me alone. This is my mica as much as it's yours, and I'm keeping it."

"Didn't you hear what that creepy guy at the store said?" I asked him. "He was right, it is fool's gold."

"You're both wrong," he said. He took out the clipboard. "Now if you'll excuse me, I have some mica to recount."

For dinner my mom made lamb chops with applesauce, the only meal I kinda look forward to, only because it's like having dinner and dessert at the same time. But then afterward you get dessert, too, which is why I secretly call it double-dessert night.

"That's enough," she said as I scooped more applesauce onto my plate. "You've only had two bites of your lamb chops and six scoops of applesauce."

"Lady, you're the one who made the meal," I said, forcing myself to eat a piece of lamb chop. It caught in my throat and I made a fake hacking sound. "See? I need the applesauce because it helps the meat go down."

"Just drink some water," Dad said.

I made a big show of it, cutting up my lamb chops into really tiny cubes, and then chewing on them ninety times apiece. Sunny stared at me with her mouth open.

"So why don't each of you tell us one interesting thing you learned in school today," Mom suggested.

"I'll go first. In science class we learned about eutrophication," Sunny said. "It's when a lake builds up nutrients and so there's excess plant growth, which is why year after year Frost Lake is getting smaller!"

"That has to be the boringest thing I've ever heard in my life," I said, winking at my dad, but he didn't wink back.

"Don't be rude, Peter. Honey, that's very interesting," Mom said, before turning to me. "How about you?"

I thought about every class I'd had that day, but I hadn't paid any attention during any of them because I was so busy collecting stuff. It wasn't fair—Sunny was already queen of the school and could actually focus on her classes and stuff happening all around her, while I had to do extra work just to remind people that I even existed. I racked my brain but couldn't remember a single second of anything my teachers had said, besides gushing about how amazing Sunny was.

"In science class we learned about, um . . . hair," I finally said.

"We never learned about hair in science class," Sunny said, with a suspicious look on her face. "But I know everything about it."

"Well, they must have realized they didn't teach your grade the right things and have been changing the curriculum," I said. "Did you know that even kids lose hair?"

"Of course," Sunny said. "Humans have between 100,000 and 150,000 hair follicles on their scalps. The hairs grow back when you lose them."

That's another annoying thing about Sunny. Anytime I try to say anything, she jumps on it to prove that she's already an expert on the topic, so I didn't ask her what a follicle was, even though I was really curious.

"And then in my other classes I found a ton of hair on the carpets at school," I went on. "Janitors collect them in these human hairballs, and I was thinking maybe for my invention I could set up a factory where they straighten it out and glue it together to make wigs. That way we wouldn't waste the hair that we lose."

"That's the stupidest idea I've ever heard in my life," she replied.

"Well, I like that it's giving you ideas for inventions," Dad said.

I was grateful that he backed me up, but my good feelings toward my dad only lasted a few minutes. After dinner he laid a bombshell on me, as if the first day of school hadn't been upsetting enough. Now that I was in middle school, he expected me to spend two hours every night after dinner studying, and even worse, I couldn't watch TV or play video games until after study time was over!

I sat at my desk looking at the class outlines I'd received, and then flipped through the two textbooks I'd brought home. I'd left the rest of the books in my locker back at school. I opened my notebooks, but of course they were completely empty.

Ten minutes later my mom checked in on me and saw me staring at the wall.

"Peter, let's focus now," she said. Then she went into Sunny's room, and I heard her mutter, "Wow, your notebooks are almost a third full already, and it's only the first day of school!"

"Do they give out a medal for that?" I muttered, but they didn't hear me. I pictured Sunny in her room, beaming up at my mom, and it made my ears burn. I reminded myself that deep down Sunny was jealous: In order to be the queen of everything, she had to spend all her free time busting her butt just to hold on to the position, while I could coast and get the same grades.

Mom left Sunny's room, so I quickly opened up a note-book and started scribbling random numbers in it. When she reentered my room, I held my arm out stiffly, as if I was trying to maintain deep concentration. I even closed my eyes, and started muttering. "Okay, square root of 3, minus the subtotal of negative 42, carry over the x, and—"

I peeked out of the corner of my eye and saw that she was backing out of the room with a smile on her face. When she was gone, I stopped pretending and looked down at the paper. I hadn't been paying attention as I scribbled, and across the top of the page it read:

$$3+3+3+3+3+3+3+3+3+$$

I continued pretending I was doing homework for a couple minutes. I wrote random numbers down on the page and kept babbling made-up formulas and stuff. It was kinda fun to pretend at first, but it turns out that faking doing homework is actually really tiring, and I wondered if it would be less of a hassle to just do my homework for real. But since I hadn't written down the assignments, I couldn't test out this theory, even if I'd wanted to. So instead I put down my pen, sat back, and just thought about the day, and how things had gone so horribly, and it made me feel bummed again. To make myself feel better, I thought about my life before sixth grade started, back when me and Drew were kings. Next thing I knew, I was daydreaming about my family's trip to Maine last summer.

We'd rented a summerhouse for a week, and my parents loved hearing the waves out their bedroom window every night so much that when they came home, they bought a sound machine at Target. It's this little plastic box that you plug in next to your bed, and it has these different settings for relaxing sounds that help you sleep. You can listen to a recording of a rainstorm all night, or crickets, or the one my parents love—the sound of waves crashing on the shore. They got it so it would make them feel like they live next to the ocean year-round, and now they can't sleep without it. I know this because my dad went on a business trip earlier this year and complained that he couldn't sleep because he missed the sound of fake waves crashing onto the bedside table.

I bolted upright in my seat and took out my inventions notebook, because I suddenly had an idea for a new one. Maybe I could make a sound machine for people who miss living in the city! Carson moved here from Manhattan in third grade, and he always used to complain that Fenwick was way too quiet. Even though he'd already been here for a year before I moved in, he was still always whining about how naturey it is out here, because I think it makes him feel cool, being from the city. My version of the sound machine would make sleeping out in the sticks feel like home for city people. There would be three settings on the dial:

Car Alarm
Opera Singer
Home Invasion

A city person could set it to "Car Alarm," and all night long they'd enjoy a deep sleep as the machine imitated the sound of a car alarm outside going off all night long down the street. "Opera Singer" would be that annoying opera singer who practices singing her scales at all hours of the night and who seems to live next door to everyone in the city, according to the movies. "Home Invasion" would be for those nights you really have trouble sleeping out in the country. You turn the dial up and fall asleep to the sound of glass breaking, followed by menacing footsteps coming from the kitchen. "And it will be called . . . the Urban Sound Machine," I whispered. Apparently I brainstormed the invention for two straight hours, because the next thing I knew, my dad was standing at the door.

"You look wired," he said. "I think you've worked hard enough tonight. Why don't you brush your teeth and go to sleep."

I hate brushing my teeth—it always puts me in a foul mood when I'm forced to do it—and this time it made me remember how horrible things were at school. Usually I play video games before bed because it helps me have funner dreams, but I felt so depressed that I voluntarily got into bed extra early for the first time ever. It wasn't even nine p.m., but I just lay there, staring up at the ceiling, trying to cheer myself up by telling myself that I might have just come up with the invention that would win the competition. And as for the situation at school, at least things couldn't get worse.

I was wrong about that last part.

eight

THE NEXT MORNING DREW AND I stood in the lobby torturing ourselves by watching everyone enjoy each other's company. Drew looked like he was about to cry. "I know you're bummed," I told him, "but it's going to take a little time. We'll figure out how to change things around, but it's not going to happen overnight. It's like grass seeds . . . you don't just plant them and then immediately watch the grass sprout, right? You have to be patient, and water the seeds every day, and then eventually the grass starts to grow."

"How do we water our seeds?"

"I don't know, I just came up with that," I admitted.

"Now I really have to pee," Drew said.

I have this weird disease where if someone says they have

to pee, it makes me immediately have to pee, too, so we headed over to the bathroom next to the main lobby. The second we stepped inside, we realized our fatal error: The Sweet brothers were standing over by the sinks.

"Hey, it's that kid, Pete," Hugh said to his twin brother, Hank, before draping a meaty arm around my shoulder. I was shocked at how heavy it was. "You're Sunny Lee's little brother, right?"

"Uh-huh," I said quickly, hoping my relationship to the queen of the school would get us out of trouble.

"I hate Sunny Lee," Hugh continued, and put me in a headlock from behind. "I bet you're a goody-goody just like her, huh? Ruining the curve in class for everybody, winning everything, president of all the clubs?"

"No, I hate her, too!" I tried to shout, but he had me pinned, and my own left arm was blocking my nose and mouth. "Drew, tell him!"

"It's true," Drew said. "They aren't close at all! They should be going to family counseling."

I stared at Drew. He shrugged.

"Who asked for your opinion?" Hugh snapped at him.

"Nobody," Drew squeaked. "My mom says I speak out of turn all the time."

"What's your name?"

"Duh-duh-rew," he stuttered.

"Well, Doo Doo Roo, congrats, you two just made the list."

"What list?" Drew asked.

This made the Sweet brothers angry.

"Now you made the top of the list!" Hank snarled.

"And again, this list is . . . ?" Drew asked.

"Shut up, Drew!" I managed to shout.

"We're going to make you wish you didn't go to Fenwick Middle," Hank said, shoving Drew against the wall.

"We already kinda wish that, so you don't have to bother," I explained between gasps for air.

"Boy, you two don't know when to keep your mouths shut," he said, and shoved Drew against the wall again.

"Why'd you shove me again?" Drew wailed.

"I guess you were just closer," he replied. For a guy generally considered to be one of the dumbest kids ever, I had to admit he had a decent handle on common sense.

"We'll be seeing you two around," Hugh said.

And then they left. I fell to my knees and took in huge lungfuls of air.

"Are you okay, Pete?" Drew asked.

"I think I almost just choked to death."

Drew patted me on the back.

"Well, at least it's over," he said.

It didn't cheer me up because he was only halfway right.

It was over but only temporarily. (I've gotten food sickness twice in my life, and the second time it happened I'd learned to not be happy after I threw up, because I knew I was just going to boot twenty minutes later.) I turned to Drew. "Did you hear what they said, though? They hate Sunny! At least someone at this school doesn't worship her."

Drew cracked a half smile. Then his face got all scrunched up.

"So what's this list Hugh kept talking about earlier?"

"Are you serious?" I shouted.

Drew was walking really slowly on the way home, focusing on his shoes.

"What are you doing?" I asked, matching his pace. "Are we having a slowest-walker race? You know you have to announce it before it starts, or else it isn't fair."

"The slower we walk, the longer it takes to get to Corbett Canyon, and the longer it takes for tomorrow to come," he said, not looking up at me.

"Buddy, I don't think time works that way," I explained.

"I know, but it makes me feel a little better to do this," he said, and stopped. "I can't believe we now have the Sweet brothers after us. It's like one problem after another."

"Well, there is one thing we could do that might solve things," I said.

"What's that?"

I sighed.

"As much as I hate to do this, we could try to glom on to my sister, and people will start respecting us, since she's the queen of the school."

Now Drew sighed.

"The Sweet brothers hate her, remember?"

"That's just the Sweet brothers, because they're bad at school, so of course they hate her. But all the teachers worship her, and everyone knows she's the star of everything."

"Do you think it would really work?"

"Think of it this way: It's like being one of those little fishes that hang on to the bellies of great white sharks in those Animal Planet videos. They eat the barnacles or whatever on the sharks, and all the other fishes that get eaten by great whites respect these little fishes because they're in tight with the great whites. The little fishes hate great whites just like all the other fishes, but they swallow their pride in order to take advantage of them. We can be those little fishes!"

"But you can't stand Sunny—would you really be able to do this?"

"I have no choice at this point. This is business, not personal."

"Okay."

"That's the spirit," I said. "So, starting next week, we'll just hang all over her whenever we see her in school, to remind everyone that I'm her brother and you're her brother's best friend."

On Monday Drew and I paced back and forth outside the band room before homeroom, waiting for Sunny's rehearsal to end.

"Why don't they play more modern music?" Drew asked me.

"How many modern songs do you know that feature the tuba?" I said.

"Good point."

The bell rang, and Sunny was the first one out of the room. Immediately Drew took her flute case from her.

"Here, buddy," he said. "Let me carry that thing for you. Boy, it's heavy!"

An eighth-grade trombone player snickered behind us.

"Hey, everybody, this wimp thinks a flute's heavy!" he shouted, and Sunny's bandmates laughed.

"I'll carry your schoolbag," I offered, but she turned her back so I couldn't pull it off her.

"What are you two doing?" she said.

Drew beamed at her.

"We're just being helpful, Sunny, since you're my BEST

FRIEND'S SISTER," he said loudly, looking at the rest of the band kids.

"I don't need the help," she snapped, grabbing her flute back and heading in the opposite direction.

I watched her walk off. I couldn't believe we were being forced to pretend to actually like a monster like that. Drew put a hand on my shoulder.

"Well, we tried," he said.

"Give it time," I said. "If there's one thing I know about Sunny, it's that she loves to have people drool all over her."

"Gross!"

"It's just a figure of speech."

"I know it is, but I couldn't help picturing it."

I groaned. "Thanks a lot, now I'm picturing everyone drooling all over Sunny, too!"

"It's a gross picture, right?"

"Maybe we should stop talking for a little while," I said, squinting the image out.

Anytime we saw Sunny at school that day, we'd practically sprint at her, and in response she started dodging us whenever she saw us. It didn't matter, the plan wasn't working anyway. We made a big show of knowing her whenever we managed to catch up to her, but nobody seemed to even take notice. And meanwhile, for the first time I was realizing that Sunny might have been the best student, the president of all the clubs, and worshipped by all the teachers, but that was different from being popular. She was always heading off to class or her locker or the library between periods, never stopping to chat with friends. Nobody called her over as she marched to the library after seventh period, and I wondered if maybe it wasn't just the Sweet brothers who weren't friends with her.

By the end of the day I was sick of trying to act like I actually liked her, and at dinner Sunny started complaining about it to Mom and Dad.

"He's following me everywhere," she whined. "It's annoying."

"Your brother just wants to be near you in school," Mom said, smiling at me.

I tried very hard not to throw up a little in my mouth and pretended she was right. I nodded, even though it made me feel gross to do it.

"It would be nice if my own sister liked to spend time with her brother," I said.

"You're a loser, though."

"I'm a loser? The Sweet brothers hate you!"

"Of course they do—they're nobodies!" She laughed. "They're probably going to be in the eighth grade for the next ten years."

I thought about it for a second.

"What about everyone else in school?" I asked. "How come I never see you hanging out with anyone between classes?"

Sunny glared at me.

"Your sister's involved in so many clubs, not to mention so focused on studies, that I'm sure she doesn't have time to loiter in the hallways between classes," Mom suggested.

Sunny nodded, still glaring at me.

"You go ahead and be like the Sweet brothers, and I'll be sure to visit the three of you at whatever gas station you work at in ten years," she said.

"The odds of all of us working at the same gas station in ten years is—"

"Enough! Why do I even bother trying to eat anymore?" Dad suddenly shouted. He very carefully put his uneaten forkful of steak on the plate and stared at my mom. "Honey, are they too old to put up for adoption?"

Mom laughed.

"You signed up for this job, too, mister," she said.

"No, I didn't! When you asked about having kids, I suggested getting a dog."

"Do you guys realize you're talking out loud?" I asked them.

nine

THE NEXT MORNING AT SCHOOL, Sunny suddenly started acting differently around us. She didn't complain when Drew offered to carry her schoolbag to homeroom, and before second period she even showed up at my locker and asked if I'd bring her flute down to the band room for her. Before every period she found us and let us run errands for her: carrying her books, shutting her locker for her, sharpening pencils for her before class started . . . and it wasn't until lunch that I realized what she was doing.

"Forget this," I said, after me and Drew had raced down to the vending machine outside the cafeteria to buy her a bag of chips. "She's not trying to be a decent sister, she's just using us for slave labor."

"What kind of a person would do such a thing?" Drew

asked, his face all twisted up as if he'd bitten into an apple with a worm in it. "That's so deceptive."

We caught up to her in the hallway—and I made a big show of opening up the bag of chips right in front of her and eating a couple, then offering some to Drew, who chomped loudly right in front of her face.

"We're eating your chips, what are you going to do about it?" Drew asked.

"You paid for them with your own money, so I'm totally fine with it," she said, and headed into her class.

"It's also kinda lame that she always has to have the last word on everything," he added.

I sighed.

At lunch Drew and I were miserable. "I really want to get an ice cream, but I spent all my extra dough on those chips," I whined.

"I don't want to sound the alarm bells too early, but it might be time to start thinking about running away," Drew suggested.

"I don't think we're there yet, but I'll take your suggestion under consideration."

"There goes another scheme down the drain. . . . I can't believe this is happening to us," he said. "Do you think we're being punished for something?"

"You mean by God?" I asked. Drew nodded. "I don't think so. We didn't do anything wrong. And I go to church every Easter. That better count for something. Where's this coming from, anyway?"

"We were popular last year. Maybe that's why this is happening."

"Being popular isn't a crime. And we weren't mean to people like they are to us. I was always nice to Carson, for example. Remember that time in fifth grade when I let him eat some of my Tater Tots at lunch?"

Drew's eyes lit up.

"I remember that day," he said. "He didn't even ask, you just offered them to him totally out of the blue. You didn't have to do that."

"I know, I was being nice!" I said.

"So, what then? Is it just bad luck?"

I shrugged my shoulders.

"I have to pee," Drew said.

"Do you tell me that because you know it's going to make me have to pee, too, or do you just really want me to know?"

Drew thought about it for a second.

"I guess a bit of both."

I sighed. We ditched our lunch trays and went to the bathroom off the lobby. Of course, the Sweet brothers were standing by one of the sinks, filling it with wet paper towels.

"Hey, boys, we've been looking for you two!" Hank said.

"Do these guys even go to class?" I whispered to Drew.

"We really have to stop using this bathroom," he whispered back, and I glared at him.

"Actually, I left my wallet in the cafeteria," I announced, starting to back out.

"Oh darn, I did, too," Drew said.

"Everyone else keeps them in their back pockets," I told him.

"Yes, that does make more sense—oof," Drew said, bumping into the wall as we headed for the door. "Let's now go get our wallets and put them in our back pockets so in the future—"

"Hold it!" Hugh shouted.

We froze.

"Now come forward," Hank said.

We did. It was like they had invisible remote controls for us or something. And then they gave us our very-first-ever atomic wedgies. The elastic band of my underwear actually snapped in half, and the Sweet brothers laughed.

"See you soon," they said, high-fiving on the way out.

"You know, I've always been scared of getting a wedgie, but that didn't really hurt at all, I have to admit," Drew said.

"Why's your voice so high all of a sudden?" I asked.

Drew shrugged. I stared at my reflection in the mirror as

I tucked the elastic band back into my pants.

"What are we going to do about this, Peter?" he asked. "I mean, forget about becoming popular, I now just want to make it out of sixth grade alive."

Next to the mirror was a poster for the talent show, being held that coming Friday. I'd gone the last two years because Sunny played her flute for the show. She won both times. Suddenly it dawned on me that I was staring at the solution to all our problems.

"Drew, I think I just figured out a way we could kill two birds with one stone."

"What are you talking about?"

I looked at him.

"We're going to win the talent show."

I watched a smile slowly form on his face. It was like watching the sun rise.

"That's a great idea!" Drew shouted, but then his smile faded. "What's wrong?"

"Sunny always wins the talent show! No matter what we do, she'll win, because she plays the flute like a pro."

Drew twisted his mouth for a couple of seconds.

"Well, then maybe we can join her act and win the thing with her?"

"I told you I'm done trying to be nice to her!"

"What choice do we have?" he asked.

I didn't say anything. Drew was right. Maybe Sunny wasn't as popular as I'd assumed, but she was still the most important student in the school because she got the best grades, was the president of so many clubs, and won the talent show every year. To win it with her would only make everyone think we were important, too, which would at least be a step in the right direction.

After school Drew came over to my house and we went up to my bedroom, where I converted my bottle-rocket launcher back into a recorder. Then we went downstairs and snuck up on Sunny as she was practicing the flute. I started trying to play along with my recorder while Drew started hitting my old lunch box like it was a tambourine— it was really loud, and startled Sunny. Old bread crumbs from really good sandwiches from my past sprinkled out of the lunch box onto the carpet like snow.

"What do you think you're doing?" she asked us.

"Oh man, this sounds great, why didn't we think of this before?" Drew said, banging away at the lunch box. "We could probably get a record deal if we played for the right people."

"You know, Sunny, Drew has a point there," I said. "We should perform together at the talent show on Friday. I heard that talent scouts from Hollywood will be in the audience."

"There is no chance we'll play together," she sniffed. "You guys are horrible."

"What are you talking about?" I said, and started rocking out on my recorder again. Sunny rolled her eyes.

"Do you even know any other songs besides 'Three Blind Mice?'" she asked.

I sighed. In order for her to need my help someday, I'd need to actually have something to offer her.

"I was thinking you could play a fancy version of it with us."

"Leave me alone, you're wasting my time," she said, and we trudged out of the living room. We went over to Drew's house and got online to the school's website to sign up for the talent show, even though we didn't even have an act for it, and that's when we saw the Lost-and-Found Forum for the first time. At the top it read:

Have you lost something? Post an alert here in the official Fenwick Middle School Lost-and-Found Forum!

Below it there was already a half dozen posts from students.

Reply to: Heidi Markowitz <hmarkovitz@easynote.com>
I lost my iPod this morning (Friday, September 7). It is

a black 160GB with hard clear plastic case—either in the music room or on bus 17.

Email me if you have found my phone.

Reward offer!

And:

Reply to: Hank Sweet <*hsweet@zebramail.com*>

My Notre Dame hat missing. If you find it, immediately return it or else. Hank Sweet.

"At least we haven't lost anything in school," Drew said.

"You're a really positive person, you know that?" I told him.

He smiled at me.

"Well, I eat right," he said.

"That doesn't make any sense," I replied.

We tried to figure out what we could do for an act. It was kinda depressing to realize that, outside of collecting mica, we weren't really that good at anything else.

I sighed.

"Isn't there anything else we're good at besides collecting?" I asked Drew.

"I have that magic set in my bedroom from a long time ago."

"Now, there's a start. Let's check it out," I said, trying to feel hopeful.

Unfortunately it was a basic kid's set—just a bunch of stupid coin tricks and some colored scarves for beginner-level juggling.

"Coin tricks aren't nearly exciting enough. Where'd you get this, anyway?"

"At the pawnshop."

"Maybe they have advanced sets or something."

We rode our bikes over to the pawnshop. The creepy owner was sitting behind the cash register, reading an issue of *Guns & Ammo*.

"Do you have any advanced magic sets?" I asked him. "Something that involves a lot of smoke and stuff? Or something that would cause a really huge but safe explosion?"

He led us to the back of the store, where there were two aisles full of magic stuff: a magician's hat and wand, some used kids' sets just like the one Drew already owned. I groaned. Drew noticed a weird jacket hanging from a hook at the end of the aisle.

"What's that?" he asked.

"An authentic straitjacket from an old asylum," the store owner said.

"What's a straitjacket?" I asked.

"They keep mental patients in them so they don't bite their arms off."

"Yuck," Drew said.

"But what the heck does that have to do with magic?" I asked. "Shouldn't that be in the insane-asylum aisle?"

"It's an old magic trick—Houdini used to escape from one hanging upside down. After two minutes you run the risk of getting brain damage."

"Perfect!" I said. "I have a pretty big brain, so I can afford to lose plenty of brain cells. How much?"

"It's for an adult, so it's too big for you," he said, hanging the jacket back on the rack.

"Even better," I said. "That'll make it easier to get out of."

"We don't do returns here. I don't want your parents coming in here mad at me for selling you something you can't use."

"So you're trying to talk us out of buying it?" Drew asked. "What kind of a salesman are you?"

The owner stared at us for a couple of seconds and realized we were dead serious. Then he took the straitjacket back down, and we followed him up to the register. Drew also bought the magician's wand and hat, along with a red plastic cape from an incomplete, used Superman costume. We immediately brought our loot back to Corbett Canyon and spent an hour putting the straitjacket on each other.

There were all these straps, but we figured out that if you kept it loose enough you could squirm out of it, eventually.

The rest of the week we went straight to Corbett Canyon after school each day to work on our act. Drew prepared his spiel as the magician, while I kept practicing getting out of the straitjacket on my own. I got good enough at it that I figured I could do it just as easily upside down. On Thursday afternoon we met with the janitor and he helped us set things up on the stage of the auditorium. The act would require that I use a harness (which the janitor had because he used it for cleaning the windows on the second floor of the school) tied to my feet so I could hang upside down. By the time Friday night rolled around, we were convinced that our act could beat Sunny's boring flute performance and solve all of our problems.

ten

THE AUDITORIUM AT SCHOOL WAS already packed when we showed up for the talent show Friday night. Everyone in school was there, along with everyone's parents. I could see my mom and dad in the third row, looking through the program. Sunny was up last, while we were the fourth act. I felt nervous peeking out at the packed audience and just wanted to get the act over with, but there was a delay when the third act—a seventh-grade girl in a pink tutu, couldn't find her ballet shoes and ended up having to do the dance in her sneakers. At one point she tried to stand on her tippy toes and almost fell into the first row. When it was finally our turn, the janitor helped set up the act behind the closed curtains.

He'd secured a rope to the metal girder above the stage,

and we positioned a ladder directly underneath it. I climbed up the ladder, sat on the top, and put on the straitjacket. Drew secured the straps, and then we attached the rope to the harness around my legs. When Drew was in position offstage, we gave the janitor the thumbs-up, and he cranked the curtain open. The crowd murmured as I waved at everyone from atop the ladder in the center of the stage. Drew walked out into the middle of the stage, wearing the cape and magician's hat, waving the plastic wand in his right hand.

"People of Fenwick!" Drew shouted. "Many of you don't know me and my partner Peter yet, because this is our first year at the middle school, but my name is Drew Newmark, and in addition to being best buddies with Peter Lee, who's sitting right up there—hi, Peter!—in addition to being best friends, we're also . . . practicing musicians!"

"Magicians," I corrected him.

"Magicians!" Drew said. "Anyway, our hero is David Blaine. Growing up we were obsessed with his bootleg 'street magic' videos, and he inspired us to study all the masters. So today we're going to re-create one of Houdini's most famous acts. As you can see, Peter is trapped in a real straitjacket, which they use in mental asylums so the patients don't bite their own arms off. On the count of three, Peter's going to hang upside down from this girder and escape from this straitjacket, but it's very risky. He'll have to do it in under two minutes, because after that an upside-down human starts to lose brain cells, and he could black out and get serious brain damage."

The principal and vice-principal stared up at me from the first row with shocked looks on their faces.

"Okay, here we go, this is very dangerous—one, two three!"

And then Drew shoved the ladder away and I immediately swung upside down, and my head banged against the ladder really hard, and everyone in the auditorium muttered "Oof," and I shouted, "I'm okay, ouch, okay, look at the clock on the wall, I have two minutes before brain damage starts setting in," and I started furiously squirming in the straitjacket.

It was actually pretty awesome at first. In twenty seconds I got one arm free, and the audience cheered. The plan was working!

"I taught him that move," I heard Drew say. He looked up at me. "You're doing great, buddy, just keep squirming the way I taught you. That's it. . . ."

But then something went wrong. Well, what went wrong is that nothing else happened. The more I struggled, the more the straps tightened, and I couldn't dislodge my right arm, and my left hand couldn't undo any of the straps.

A minute and a half passed, then two minutes.

"As Peter spins around during his struggle, you can see that his cheeks are turning pink, and now you'll notice that his forehead is visibly darkening as well," Drew said to a stunned audience.

This made me panic, and I started struggling harder. Principal Curtis looked over at the janitor, motioning for him to help me out.

"I'm fine," I screamed, practically out of breath, and the janitor took his hands off the ladder, as if it was boiling hot. I started twisting harder, and I could feel my face turning purple. A couple of seconds later I officially blacked out and went limp. According to Drew, my eyes became pure whites, since my pupils were drifting into the back of my head, and the audience gasped. The janitor then rushed up the ladder, pulled off the harness, carried the now unconscious me down, and unstrapped me from the straitjacket. I suddenly came to and immediately started struggling to free myself from the straitjacket again, even though I was no longer wearing it, and then I realized the janitor was on top of me, and in a panic I punched him in the nose. The principal nearly had a heart attack considering the future lawsuits he'd be facing for having allowed a Fenwick student to pass out hanging upside down from the rafters in a straitjacket during the annual talent show, and it was somewhere around this point when everyone in the auditorium started laughing like crazy. Drew groaned when he heard one of the Sweet brothers holler, "Give it up for Street Magic and Street Magic's Assistant, everybody!" and everyone started chanting a new nickname:

"Street Magic! Street Magic!"

By the time the next act finally went on (after a short delay while the gym teacher forced me to inhale smelling salts even though I was already resuscitated), Drew and I had slunk over to this empty room that had a cardboard sign on the door that read GREENROOM. The room wasn't actually green, so I felt like I had the right to swipe the sign down and rip it into a million pieces because it made me feel better. Drew locked the door and sat down next to me. I was so mad that I refused to talk to him at first.

"Say something, Peter," he said. "I get the feeling you're upset with me."

This made me explode, and I shoved him in the chest.

"You made the straps too tight!"

"No, I didn't!"

Drew started bawling, and I had no choice but to console him, even though I was still furious with him because I have this embarrassing disease (similar to my peeing disease) where if anyone near me cries long enough, I end up crying, too. I guess my mom has a point when she says I'm so emotional. Whenever I cry, she instantly bear-hugs me and refuses to let go, even if we're out in public, saying things like, "Don't ever change, Son," and "You're so brave to let it out!"

"Now everyone's going to think I'm friends with a magician." I sighed.

Now he shoved me in the chest.

"What are you talking about? This was your idea!" he screamed. "Everyone's going to call me Street Magic from now on."

"You're the one who claimed to be a magician!" I replied, but he started getting teary-eyed again, so I immediately switched gears. "Take it easy, buddy, it's actually a cool nickname. You sound like a new Transformer or something."

He smiled at me.

"Thanks, Peter," he said. "You're my best friend."

I sighed.

"No, Drew, I'm your *only* friend, remember?" I corrected him.

"Well, you're that, too," he replied.

Outside we heard laughter in the audience. I opened the door and we crept over to the side of the stage. Sunny was trying to play her flute, but all the kids in the audience were laughing and talking as if she wasn't there. I heard the occasional "Street Magic" and blushed.

"Everybody, quiet down!" Ms. Schoonmaker, the host for the talent show, shouted into a mic as she bounded across the stage. "Let's give each performer the same due respect. Sunny, why don't you start over."

Sunny's face was bright red. The crowd finally quieted down, and she started playing her piece again; she looked as if at any moment she was going to bite the flute in half. She didn't have any reason to be mad, though, because she ended up winning a third time anyway, which sealed our fate.

"It's been nice knowing you," I said to Drew when it was all over.

There was a reception out in the lobby afterward with tables full of cookies and treats, but Drew's mom grabbed him and made him leave immediately, and Sunny headed straight for the car, so we had to leave, too. I looked back sadly at all the desserts. During the car ride home, Sunny completely lost it with me.

"You ruined my performance!" she screamed.

"Are you crazy? Who cares, you won the contest!" I shook my head at her. "It saddens me, really, to see firsthand just how spoiled great whites can be."

"Great whites?" Sunny said. "Are you even on this planet right now?"

"Sunny, I know you're upset," Mom said soothingly. "But

Peter's right, you did win the contest again."

Sunny glared at me.

"I hate you," she muttered.

"I think you're giving yourself permanent wrinkles by glaring all the time," I said back to her.

"Knock it off, you two," Dad said, rubbing his temples with one hand as he drove with the other.

"I'm actually being serious," I said.

"Peter, just be grateful you didn't hurt yourself," he said. "And Sunny, I'm proud that you composed yourself while everyone was so loud, and still managed to play. It's a testament to—"

I stopped paying attention, because I was now picturing the Sweet brothers shouting, "Give it up for Street Magic and Street Magic's Assistant, everybody!" and having to face them on Monday. Maybe running away wasn't a bad option, after all.

eleven

"**P**ETER?" TRENT WAVED ME OVER when I stepped into the lobby at school the following Monday. He was smiling at me for once, which was surprising, but I didn't have time to really think about it because for some reason the floor was covered with a thick layer of fog.

"Is there a fire?" I asked, pointing at the fog.

"Yeah, and our classmates are trapped in the gym—let's go help them," Trent said, and we ran to the double doors and he swung them open. He started waving his arms over his head, I thought at first because he was trying to clear away the smoke, but a second later Drew walked out of the foggy gym with a serious look on his face.

Suddenly he whipped around and hollered, "Okay, everybody!"

What sounded like a fire alarm erupted overhead, and at first I thought it had to do with the smoke on the ground, but then the entire student body poured out of the gym into the lobby and mobbed me, trying to get their hands on me. At first I felt scared, like they were going to rip me into pieces, but then I realized everyone was patting me on the back.

"Surprise!" Angie shouted, beaming at me.

Trent twirled his right hand as he bowed, then pointed at a huge golden chair in the corner by the fire escape. "Your rightful throne, sire," he said in a British accent. "For far too long you have been deprived of it."

"What's happening?" I asked Drew.

"This was all an elaborate setup, buddy," he replied, clapping me on the back. "Smile at the camera, you just got punk'd!"

A camera crew stepped out from behind the fog, and everyone cheered.

"Peter?" Sally tapped my shoulder shyly. "Do you think you could make me a mica necklace? The one you gave me last year that I wear in bed every night broke."

Sally still wore my mica necklace this whole time?

"Peter?" she said, nudging my shoulder. "Peter, wake up, will you?"

"Wake up?" I waved a hand in front of her face. "I'm

staring right at you."

And then I opened my eyes and yelped. Mom was standing over me, poking me in the chest as if I was a squirrel in the middle of the road and she wasn't sure if I was dead or not. "Get out of bed, you're going to be late for school," she said.

I sighed and got out of bed. It had been such a nice dream, but it only made real life feel even worse. Plus, whenever I have a really realistic dream, it makes me feel confused for a while, like I've just run around in circles for two straight minutes.

After breakfast I tried to play sick, but Mom wasn't hearing it.

"For one thing, you just ate three bowls of cereal," she pointed out. "Surely you can't be sick if you have such a big appetite."

"Would it help my case if I barfed it all back up?" I pleaded.

"Don't be gross. Now get dressed, you're late as it is."

I met up with Drew at his house, and then we walked to school together, silently praying that the talent show hadn't made things worse. Unfortunately when we entered the lobby, it got really quiet all of a sudden and everyone stared at us. Hugh came over and clapped me on the back.

"There's Street Magic!" he shouted, and it was like he

was turning a valve, because then everyone in the lobby started shouting our nickname.

The bell rang and we made our way over to the stairs. Angie and Sally blocked our path. "Hey, Street Magic," Angie said to Drew. "You're a magician, you don't need to take the stairs, you can just blink and reappear in home-room, right?"

Students snickered.

"Actually, I'm Street Magic's Assistant," Drew clarified. "Peter's the real Street Magic."

"Thanks for clearing that up for everyone," I whispered.

"You're welcome!"

"I was being sarcastic."

The crowd started talking again, and a minute later the homeroom bell rang. I looked over at the far wall and made eye contact with Sunny. She shook her head at me before heading up the stairs. I usually couldn't care less when people shake their heads at me, because it's always adults who do that, and I know that they're shaking their heads merely because they don't remember at all what it was like to be a kid. But for someone close to my age to do it made me so angry that it made my fingertips tingle, and I swear they looked really fat all of a sudden, as if they were going to explode. For a moment I honestly believed my finger-tips were going to detonate at any moment, and I held my breath until they looked normal again. Phew. Then I pictured what my fingertips exploding would look like, and cringed.

"Gross," I muttered, before heading up the stairs.

In math class Mrs. Ryder announced that we had a pop quiz.

"But you didn't tell us there was going to be a quiz," I cried.

"Hence the term 'pop quiz,'" Mrs. Ryder said.

"You're sneaky, Mrs. Ryder. And that is not cool. NOT COOL," I scolded her.

The surprising thing was that everyone in class laughed, thinking I was just playfully joshing around with her. I'd never offered to answer any of my teachers' questions, and whenever I got called on I'd just shrug, so technically this was my first time saying anything during class, ever, in middle school.

"You should call them sneak-attack quizzes, instead," I added, but nobody laughed.

Tough crowd, I thought.

I stared at the quiz and sighed. Technically, Sunny never had pop quizzes because she studied every night as if there was going to be one the next day. Nothing surprised her. The scary part was that I didn't recognize the math at all, but luckily it was a multiple-choice quiz, which gave me a fighting chance at doing really well. I'd overheard Sunny say to Mom when she was studying for the SATs that when you had no clue on a question, don't try to answer it, but I still guessed on some of them, just so it didn't look fishy.

The one bright spot that week was that it was finally time for my first-ever T.A.G. class, after school on Wednesday in the library. On Sunday night I'd gotten really excited about becoming an inventor, and since I had no idea there was going to be a pop quiz in math the next day, I didn't bother studying. Instead, I focused on brainstorming ideas, and came up with what I thought at the time were two doozies. The first one was a new kind of security system. I figured the problem with them was that even when they work, the family inside the house still gets totally freaked out and probably can't go back to sleep for a while, right? So my idea was called Mr. Home Security. I called it that because it's kinda like having a Mr. Coffee machine wired to your security system, except it's a teakettle in your bedroom. The water in the teakettle is always close to boiling on a hot plate at all times, and when the alarm gets tripped, instead of an alarm blaring inside your house, startling you out of bed, the alarm system instead triggers the hot plate to full blast. This quickly brings the teakettle to a boil, and you get woken up instead by the soothing sound of a tea-kettle's whistle. Then you just calmly get out of bed, lock the bedroom door so the burglar can't get inside the room and take you hostage, and then relax in bed drinking hot tea with the lights on while you wait for the local police to arrive and reset the security system.

I pictured a young couple nervously drinking their tea as they hid in the locked bedroom waiting for the police, and I figured, well, maybe one of them smokes cigarettes, especially when they're nervous. Wouldn't it be convenient, then, if cigarettes were self-lighting? I figured you could add the match-strike strip on the side of a cigarette box, and then add some chemicals to the tip of the cigarette, and then just rub the end of the cigarette against the box, and voilà, you're smoking away your worries while sipping hot tea!

This one fit under the category of "environmental/eco-friendly" inventions, according to Ms. Schoonmaker's letter, because if it really caught on, it would save:

tons of trees (matches)

gallons of gas (butane from lighters)

I glanced over at the clock by my bed. At this point, I'd spent nearly two hours coming up with ideas for inventions! I flipped through the six pages of diagrams and notes I'd already filled the notebook with and couldn't believe how

92

much work I'd gotten done. "This notebook's writing itself!" I said out loud.

On Wednesday I showed up early to the AV room in the back of the library after school, and Sunny was already sitting there, scribbling furiously in her notebook. I sat down at the other end of the long table. "Class hasn't started yet, so what could you possibly be taking notes on?" I asked.

"I'm working on my ideas," she said, not looking up. "You should be, too."

"Actually, I've been working on them all day," I said.

"You're lying—how could you? You have classes all day."

"I guess classes are easier for me than they are for you, after all," I said.

She frowned at me.

A minute later the other students filed in. There were eight of us in the class: me, Carson, and Angie were the three sixth graders in class; Leigh and Graham were seventh graders; and Sunny, Sam, and Courtney were in eighth. Carson was really smart, but I was just relieved that his buddy from Hemenway—the one with the gigantic head—wasn't selected. That kid was the only person in my grade that I worried about, intellectually.

Ms. Schoonmaker then showed up, carrying a folder and a tiny cup of steaming espresso. I love the smell of coffee, but I've always hated the smell of espresso. It's bitter and strong and smells like adults. This tiny cup filled up the entire room with the gross smell within seconds.

"Good afternoon, future inventors!" she said. "Well, there's not a moment to spare. In late October we're going to have an inventors' fair of our own, where you'll present a prototype—that is, a working example of your actual invention—to the student body. Then a committee will decide which one of you will represent the school at nationals in the spring.

"This room is going to be your official inventions workshop," Ms. Schoonmaker went on. "I've set up these cubbies where you can store your projects. During your free time before or after school, you can come to the workshop to work on your inventions. But right now we're going to start out with an exercise to get your creative minds working."

She passed out pieces of paper. On the page was a white oval in the center. The objective was to try to make some kind of creative picture using the white oval. I sat there for a few minutes just staring at the page. Everyone else was drawing furiously, but nothing was coming to me!

"Two minutes left," Ms. Schoonmaker said.

My hands were sweaty. I looked at the white oval. What did it look like? With a minute left an idea finally dawned on me, and I hurried to get my picture drawn.

"Time's up," Ms. Schoonmaker said. "Now what have we come up with?"

We went around describing our pictures. All the other students, including Sunny, had done one of two things: they either turned their white eggs into spiders by adding eight legs, or they made it an egg in an Easter basket. I groaned, clearly I'd done the assignment wrong. And worse—I peeked at Sunny's page—her spider of course looked like an entry in an encyclopedia.

"Mine's really accurate because I did a report on spiders last year—the white oval is the opisthosoma, but then I went ahead and drew its cephalothorax, too," Sunny bragged.

"That is certainly very realistic," Ms. Schoonmaker agreed.

Sunny seemed pleased. As we went around describing our pictures, my throat started tightening up, as if I'd swallowed an angry bee. I casually slid my picture under the desk and crumpled it up as softly as possible right before they got to me.

"How about you, Peter?" Ms. Schoonmaker finally asked.

"I couldn't come up with anything," I said. "In fact, I'm not even sure where my paper is at the moment. That's strange."

Sunny shook her head at me. Everyone looked kind of embarrassed for me, but luckily the bell rang for the late bus.

"Okay, so from now on the class will be held every Wednesday right after school in this room. For next class, I want you to prepare a two-minute speech about one of your ideas for inventions, and then we'll analyze them."

Everyone got up to leave.

"Hey, wait a sec—where's my scarf?" Angie said, looking under the desk.

"You don't want to miss your bus, I'll do a clean sweep before I leave. You can check with me tomorrow morning," Ms. Schoonmaker said, before turning toward me. "Peter, can I speak with you for a moment?"

I blushed. Sunny shook her head at me again as she left with everyone.

"Can I see your drawing?" Ms. Schoonmaker asked.

"I did it wrong, though," I said.

She held her hand out and smiled at me. I slowly pulled out the crumpled paper. Instead of making it an Easter egg or a spider, I'd just colored the oval black with my pencil and drawn a stupid square around it. Underneath it I'd written a caption like in a newspaper cartoon: "Harold, the dog got in front of the camera again!" as if it was a picture of a dog's nose ruining a family photo. Ms. Schoonmaker looked at it for a couple of seconds before nodding.

"I had a feeling you'd come up with something special," she said.

"You mean the bad kind of 'special,' right?"

She shook her head, smiling at me.

"That everyone drew Easter eggs or spiders is fine, but those are typically the first things we think of when we see the oval. Yours shows creativity," she said. "You're already thinking outside the box. Do you know what that means?"

"Well, clearly, I'm not in a box right now," I said.

"No, it's an expression, and it means to think creatively, which you do."

I would have taken it as a compliment, but the one thing worse than the smell of espresso is the smell of espresso in someone's mouth after they've sipped a tiny cup of it, and she was breathing right in my face. She must have thought I looked nervous, but really I was just holding my breath.

"So relax! Don't stress about showing your ideas in the future, okay?"

I wasn't listening to her at this point, though, for Ms. Schoonmaker had accidentally given me the advice Drew and I had been searching for all this time. I was so excited that I ran all the way to Drew's house to give him the good news. Well, I ran halfway, then got winded, and half jogged the rest of the way, poking my hands into my ribs to stifle the cramps.

Drew was sitting in the tree house when I showed up. He'd laid out the mica all over the floor and was staring at it. He glanced up at me with a guilty look on his face.

"I couldn't help it," he said. "It still looks so cool to me. Am I crazy?"

"Don't worry about it," I said. "Because I have amazing news. I realized we've been thinking the old ways of doing things would make us popular in middle school, and we just have to change with the times."

"Okay!" he said really excitedly, before getting a serious look on his face. "Wait—what are you talking about?"

"I just found out in T.A.G. class that I'm really good at thinking outside the box. There are only a few people on the planet with this skill, and the others are all adults," I added, figuring it was probably true. "What that means is we have to think creatively. Being great collectors doesn't mean anything at Fenwick Middle. Carson was right, collecting stuff *is* so fifth grade. We have to come up with new ways of making our mark."

"How do we do that?"

I thought about it for a couple of seconds.

"Honestly, I have no idea, but just realizing this feels like a big step. We'll just think outside the box, and I bet we'll figure out a way to solve this. We'll finally become popular, and because of that the Sweet brothers will probably back off and pick on someone else."

Drew cheered.

"I knew you'd save us!"

* * *

"How was your first T.A.G. class?" Mom asked at dinner. "It must be exciting for you two to be in a class together for once."

"It's embarrassing," Sunny said. "Peter couldn't even do the exercise."

She handed Mom her ultrarealistic picture of a spider.

"First of all, it wasn't a drawing contest, and Sunny did it wrong like everybody else," I said. Sunny's eyes narrowed. "The point was to be creative, and everyone drew spiders and Easter baskets."

"What did you draw, Peter?" Dad asked.

"I made it look like a dog's nose ruining a photograph," I said, and my dad nodded.

"That is clever!" he said, and Sunny blushed. I felt a delicious chill run through me—apparently defeating Sunny was the most incredible feeling in the world! It was one thing for Ms. Schoonmaker to compliment me, but it felt ten times more satisfying to see my sister admit that I'd one-upped her.

"I could get used to this," I muttered.

"What's that, honey?" Mom asked.

"Oh, nothing."

Sunny frowned at me, not realizing that she was giving me a really nice present. I knew Sunny would never do what I said, so I tricked her by saying the exact opposite of what I wanted. "Please stop frowning," I pleaded, and sure enough, she glared even harder at me! This was the first time I'd ever felt like I was truly smarter than her, like I had an invisible remote control or something, so I added, "Please don't bare your teeth and growl at me."

"You're being weird," she said, and turned away from me.

I guess the batteries in my invisible remote control had run out.

twelve

THE PROBLEM WAS, NO THINKING-OUTSIDE-THE-BOX ideas came to us at first, which made the rest of the week even more frustrating; but when Drew and I showed up at school the following Monday, an opportunity finally presented itself. Practically everyone in our grade was walking around the lobby before homeroom wearing candy necklaces. "Where'd you get those?" I asked Carson.

"Everyone got them at Angie's party on Saturday," he explained.

It turned out that Angie'd had a huge boy-girl party that weekend. Drew and I listened in on some conversations in homeroom and overheard everyone talking about it. Apparently her parents planned on chaperoning parties regularly at their house from now on because they didn't want kids hanging out in dangerous places, unsupervised. It looked like we were the only ones in sixth grade not invited, because just about everyone seemed to be wearing these stupid candy necklaces that they'd gotten as door prizes or something. "Now everyone who didn't know we're nobodies will see that we don't have candy necklaces," Drew cried. "It's like they're wearing a badge or something."

He was right. But then I got an idea. "Remember what I said last week?" I asked him. "This is a perfect chance for us to think outside the box!"

Drew cocked his head to the side like a dog when you try to have a meaningful conversation with it.

"Refresh my memory about this box you're talking about," he said.

"C'mon," I said, grabbing his arm. We snuck over to the art room, where we cut pieces of yarn and made our own necklaces. Then we just walked around all morning sucking on our strings and pretending to feel bad that we'd finished all the candy. My theory was that everyone would assume we'd gone to the party and therefore assume we were cool, too. Unfortunately a real candy string necklace is made out of this thin gray, rubbery string, and all we had to work with was this fuzzy yellow yarn, so it didn't even look real.

"I have little pieces of yarn stuck in my throat," Drew said.

"Just keep licking," I whispered, even though he was right, because a couple of seconds later I coughed up a hairball.

"Well, that's a first," Drew said.

So the fake-candy-necklace idea didn't work, but at lunch Drew and I came up with different get-popular-quick schemes to trick students into thinking we were cool, and all afternoon we tried them out. Unfortunately none of them worked, because Drew wasn't very good at following the plan. The most promising idea I'd come up with was to spread a bunch of "cool" rumors about each other.

Did you hear about Peter's surgery?

or

Have you seen Drew? I know he rescued all those elderly people from the overturned bus, but . . .

I walked around real slowly all day, holding my left side, the side I'd supposedly gotten a kidney removed from, but nobody bothered to ask me what was wrong. I asked a dozen different people if they'd seen Drew, pretending to be really panicked. I said I was worried that Drew had gotten hurt internally when he saved all those old people, and like a cat he'd crawled off someplace on his own to die by himself. (Cats get embarrassed that they look undignified when they have death spasms.) But each time, the student would just go, "What are you talking about? He's standing right over there."

Sure enough, Drew would be down the hall, waving at us with a goofy smile on his face. I dragged him into the bathroom after sixth period.

"The rumor doesn't make any sense if you don't make yourself scarce, for the entire day," I yelled.

"Sorry," he said. "I keep forgetting that part. Should I hide now?"

It was too late—everyone knew the jig was up—but I let him hide in a locked stall anyway, figuring he deserved some sort of punishment for not executing the plan right.

Drew looked really pouty on the walk home from school that day.

"Look, it's not your fault that you couldn't hear the bell for class when you were hiding out in the stall all afternoon," I said, patting him on the shoulder. "Don't beat yourself up over it."

"It's not that," Drew said. "I just can't get over how suddenly this all happened. So out of the blue."

"I know," I said. "People look at us as if they don't

remember how things were for the last two years. How is that even possible?"

"It's like we've all of a sudden woken up in another town. Like it's the same town but on another planet or something, where people have no memory of what—"

But I wasn't listening to him anymore. Something he'd said had startled me. "You're a genius," I cut him off.

He blushed. Then, when I didn't say anything more, he said, "Would it make me less of a genius if I asked how?"

"It all makes sense to me now," I went on. "Look, let's consider the facts: One, everyone thinks we're losers. Two, we didn't go to Angie's big party last weekend, which we've established is proof that we're considered losers, right?"

"Okay, but I still don't get how that makes me a genius."

"I haven't gotten to that part yet! Let me ask you something, Drew. Why is it that we weren't at Angie's party?"

"Because she didn't invite us, and because we're losers?" Drew replied.

I sighed.

"Nope, it's because we're popular in *other towns*," I said, smiling. "And thanks to our busy, regional social lives, we just don't have time to hang out with our own classmates."

"Wait—seriously? Why didn't you tell me we were popular in other towns?" Drew's eyes grew wide.

I sighed again. I tend to sigh a lot around him.

"We're not, actually, but that's what we're going to make everyone else think—which will explain why we don't go to cool parties on the weekends, and why we never hang out with anyone else during school. Once people realize that everyone in our neighboring towns loves us, they'll have to think we're cool."

"But how do we do that?"

"It's easy, we just make up a second life that we have, and casually let people know about it," I said. "It's not like they can find out the truth—nobody knows anyone from those other towns."

He thought about it for a minute. Then his face lit up.

"That just might work," he said. "But how was that my idea?"

I smiled at him.

"You said it was like we'd woken up in another town," I said.

"I'm smarter than I thought," he said.

"Well, don't get too excited," I told him. "We have work to do. Tonight I want both of us to think outside the box and come up with ideas for how to make people think we're popular in other towns."

I jogged home the rest of the way.

thirteen

"SO WHAT IDEAS DID YOU come up with?" Drew asked when I showed up at his house the next morning.

"Sunny practiced the flute all night, and I couldn't concentrate at all," I said. "What annoyed me was that she already won the stupid talent show, so why's she practicing twice as hard as before?"

"Maybe she's as focused on winning in her own way as we're focused on trying to trick people into thinking we're popular," Drew said.

I stared at him for a moment.

"What are you, her shrink?" I asked, and he shrugged. "So what's your idea?"

"Mine's dumb. I thought maybe we could pretend to talk to cool people from other towns on my cell phone."

"That's actually a pretty decent idea, Drew."

"Really? So I'm finally thinking outside the box?"

"You're not quite there, yet, but you're definitely close," I said. "You still have one toe sticking inside the box."

"God, I hate boxes," he said.

"Now you're sounding like you don't know what the phrase means, again."

"Dang it."

After lunch I used Drew's cell phone to pretend I was getting the third degree from a girlfriend from another town as popular students walked by. Cell phones are banned until the end of the school day, so I made sure no teachers were around.

"But . . . yeah, but . . . I know . . . no . . . you see . . . will you just give me a . . . that's not what I . . . I told you that . . . ," I stammered. Then I sighed dramatically, rubbed my temples with my eyes closed the way Mom does after she talks to me for more than five straight minutes, and then I held the phone away from my ear, making eye contact with Angie. I rolled my eyes and made the cuckoo sign with my free hand, then put the phone back to my ear.

"I know . . . ," I said into the phone. "Look, if it makes you feel better, I'll . . . but . . . but . . . I didn't know she was your sister . . . but . . . don't worry, I don't care if your best friend wants to date me . . . I wouldn't intentionally do that to someone at a party in a town I don't even live in . . . it's not my fault—hello? Hello?"

Defeated, I stared at the phone for a couple of seconds before hanging up. I could feel Angie staring at me—it was *working!*

"Every single one," I muttered to himself. "Every girl in my life . . ."

"I'm telling a teacher that you're talking on a cell phone," she said.

We watched her walk away.

"Um, that didn't work so well, Peter," Drew said.

"Maybe if you hadn't stood next to me, smiling like crazy the entire time, it would've seemed more convincing," I scolded him.

"You really have to give me these instructions before-hand," Drew said.

Unfortunately Angie wasn't kidding. She immediately told a teacher about my cell-phone use, and the worst possible thing happened next. I got paged to visit the office a minute later and was informed that I had my first-ever detention after school. Just saying the word in my head gave me the creeps. *Detention.* Trent's friend Lance had said that the Sweet brothers were in detention all the time! Just picturing the Sweet brothers waiting for me in a darkened classroom, in the empty school after the buses took off, was enough to make me seriously consider running as hard as I could into the nearest wall—so I'd have to get airlifted to the hospital or insane asylum or something. By the afternoon everyone seemed to have heard the news, and everything people said about detention only made me feel more nervous. Carson leaned over in social-studies class when Mrs. Farley started writing on the chalkboard.

"I wouldn't go if I was you, Peter."

"Have you ever been to detention?" I asked him.

"Of course not," he replied. "But I've heard rumors. It's where the bad people go. The dangerous people."

"'Dangerous people?'" I repeated. That sounded terrifying. "Do they even go to our school?"

"Psst, Peter," Donnie Christopher, the Hemenway kid with the gigantic head, whispered. "Can I have your watch? It's not like you're surviving detention, anyway."

"Don't say that!"

"Peter!" Mrs. Farley snapped. "You already have detention, and if anyone wants to join him this afternoon, by all means, speak up."

Apparently word had spread among the teachers that I was in trouble, too.

After school I made the slow march over to room 12, where detention was held. I tried calming myself down as I walked, reassuring myself that Carson was just trying to scare me and probably no other kids would even be there. He was the last person who would know what detention was like, anyway, right? What creeped me out was that it was so empty and silent in the hallway as I walked toward my fate. Weirder still was the fact that, even though I was heading toward detention rather than trying to make my escape, I realized I was tiptoeing, even though nobody was around to hear me.

The door to room 12 was closed. I placed my right hand on the knob, but before turning it I said a little prayer to myself. "You're going to be okay," I whispered. Then I opened the door and my stomach immediately fell. The Sweet brothers were sitting in the front row! Mr. Tinsley waved me over to the front desk.

"You're late," he said. Which made sense—tiptoeing isn't exactly the fastest mode of transportation these days. "Since this is your first time, let's go over the house rules. You are to sit there and do homework. You are not allowed to get up from your seat unless I give you permission. You can talk quietly, but if I hear you over my headphones you will instantly get another detention. Understand? Now let me sign your detention slip."

I tried to communicate with my eyes that I was in serious danger, but he just scribbled his signature and stuck it in a folder, and without looking up, said, "Grab a seat."

"Well if it isn't Street Magic's Assistant," Hugh said, smiling so broadly that I could see the sides of his molars. My lord, they were going to *eat* me. "You're not alone, are you?"

"Uh-huh," I said.

Hugh and Hank looked at each other before breaking out in mad laughter.

"Oh, this is going to be fun," Hank said.

That's how evil the Sweet brothers were. I mean, I would never consider it "fun" to torture something weaker than me, because I'm not a psychopath. Like on the rare occasion when I spend a couple of minutes smushing ants with a basketball in the driveway, I don't think, Oh boy, killing these little ants is fun, yippee! It's just something kids my age do when they have a basketball and there are a lot of ants on the ground. It's embedded in our DNA, as my dad would say, that you simply have to smush them. It's more like a job, really; there's no "fun" involved—that's just twisted.

I looked over at Mr. Tinsley and he just nodded sleepily at me, totally unaware that my life was in danger. He had headphones on and was reading a book. A rubber band hit me in the back of the head. I pretended I hadn't felt it, even though it stung really bad, given the fact that Hugh was sitting approximately three feet away from me. He shot another one that clipped my ear.

"You better tie your shoes well, Street Magic's Assistant,"

he said in a normal voice, not bothering to whisper because Mr. Tinsley's headphones were blaring. "Because the second you get out that door, we're coming after you. And we'll be looking for you and Drew especially during the day—we're making you our special projects for the semester."

Basically for the entire detention I sat there three feet away from two thugs who wanted to jump me. It reminded me of an exhibit at the museum of prehistoric times—I was the mastodon frozen in midgallop while there were two frozen cavemen, forever about to chuck their spears at me. In my head I mapped out alternate escape routes. My best chance was to head straight for the stairs, bolt out the back, try to lose them in the woods, backtracking to Drew's house.

The bell rang, and I immediately bolted out of the room, but in my panic I made the wrong choice and headed down the hallway rather than over to the stairwell ten feet to my left. The Sweet brothers chased after me. They didn't say anything as they chased me down the hallway, and once again the silence kinda freaked me out. I didn't think I could outrun both of them, and I suddenly remembered this movie where a guy in a fighter jet slams on the brakes and the enemy jets fly right by—I figured I'd stop suddenly, and once they ran by I'd simply head back the other way, so right then I screeched to a halt.

Looking back, it wasn't a horrible plan—I'm smaller than them, so I probably can change directions faster, the only problem was they weren't nearly as close to me as I'd thought. Instead of being an arm's length behind me, they were more like fifteen feet behind me, and so by stopping I allowed them to catch up to me. They looked surprised.

"Um, thanks for stopping?" Hank said, confused at first that I'd suddenly given up when in reality I was pulling away from them. Since I'm a fast thinker, I thought maybe I could turn this into brownie points with him.

"You're welcome," I said, praying with my eyes open that they'd high-five me and that would be it. Instead Hugh turned me around and gave me my second-ever atomic wedgie, ripping the elastic band of my favorite pair of underwear (it was my favorite because it was the pair I was wearing when I first discovered mica, a year earlier). I let out a yelp.

"Sorry, pal," he said, clapping me really hard on the back. "It's like that reflex test at the doctor's—they hit your kneecap with that rubber mallet and your leg shoots out."

"Don't take this the wrong way, but I have absolutely no idea what you're talking about," I admitted.

"I'm just saying it's kinda like that—whenever I see your pants, I can't help but want to give you a serious wedgie," he explained.

They laughed.

"If I wore shorts, would you have the same reaction?" I asked.

"Are you being obnoxious?" Hugh said.

"No."

"Well, then the answer is yes—any kind of pants I think would do it."

"Maybe the solution is for you to stop looking at my pants," I offered, and this made Hugh really mad.

"I was about to let you go, but your big mouth got in the way again," Hugh said.

As he grabbed my shirt from behind, I shouted, "Stop looking at my pants!" and tugged away as hard as I could—and miraculously wrenched myself free. I bolted back toward the stairwell and practically launched myself into the air at the top of the stairs. I flew down the three flights and out the exit doors, positive they were going to tackle me at any moment, but when I finally looked behind me, the Sweet brothers were standing at the window on the second floor, gasping for breath and glaring at me. I didn't realize it at that moment, but I'd just made a major discovery that would help me in the future.

fourteen

W HEN I GOT TO DREW'S HOUSE, I told him what happened, and he patted me on the back. "Well, on the plus side, that shirt's going to last you a lot longer, since the collar's all stretched out," he said.

"Now's not really the time to be making lemonade," I said.

I explained what the Sweet brothers had said during detention, and we decided that we had no choice but to take martial-arts lessons immediately. The trick was going to be convincing our parents to let us learn how to become deadly weapons. I gave my parents a long spiel over dinner about how I wanted to be there for them when they got old, which meant I'd need to learn how to defend myself in the present. I thought the speech went pretty well, but at the end of it my parents were frowning.

"I don't want you using that stuff on your classmates. It can only lead to trouble."

"But I need it to be able to defend myself!"

"Violence never solves anything, Son," Dad said.

"What's the point of wars, then?" I asked. "We wouldn't be here if it wasn't for the American Revolution."

"That's different," he said, but he couldn't elaborate so I knew I was right.

I made my eyes look real big and wet, as if I was a cartoon deer or something.

"I just want to have the skills so I can defend myself," I said in as pitiful a voice as possible. I even sniffled a little. "Who's going to take care of you when you're really old, if I'm not around?"

"Is anyone picking on you?" Mom asked. "Tell me who it is, and I'll call their folks right this second and put a stop to it."

I knew she was trying to be nice, so I didn't have the heart to explain to her that this was probably the worst idea in the history of parenting.

"I just don't think taking martial-arts lessons is a good idea," Dad added. "You have all this aggression inside you."

"No, I don't!" I shouted, feeling really angry all of a sudden.

"Remember when we went to that park one time, and you kicked that dog as it ran by?" my dad asked.

"I thought it was going to bite me!"

"End of discussion, Peter," my mom said. "Honey, I have an idea. Why don't you try writing a letter to whoever is bothering you? I'm sure they'd understand."

"That's a wonderful idea," I said. "I don't know why I didn't think of it first, to just put it into words, of course . . ."

"That's the spirit," Mom said, pumping her fist.

"I think he's being sarcastic, honey," Dad said to her.

Even though Drew and I didn't have any classes with each other, I told my parents I was doing a project with him, and they let me go over to his house after dinner. I figured it wasn't lying because, technically, we were working on a project together: a project to save our own lives. We tried to work on his mom, thinking maybe if we got her on our side, she could convince my parents to let me take martial-arts lessons, but she was no better, because she's a dental assistant.

"Just win over your enemies with smiles, that's the best defense, boys," she suggested. "Because as everyone knows, smiling is infectious. Peter, do you need any floss?"

I sighed.

"No thanks, Mrs. N. I still haven't quite finished the container you gave me last week."

Drew and I went outside and started pacing back and forth under Corbett Canyon. I kicked at a tall weed sticking up out of the grass, but since I don't know martial arts, I missed.

We climbed up into the tree house. The moon was full, making the inside of the tree house glow a dull blue. I put on my nighttime reading helmet but didn't bother turning on the headlamp. The helmet is made of hard green plastic, with leather straps. My mom was so excited when she got me this ugly thing, but I have to admit it served its purpose—every weekend this past summer, I read comics late at night with it on.

"I guess I'm going to have to start wearing this stupid helmet to school for protection," I said.

"We're dead meat," Drew said. "And there's so much I never got to do in my life . . . I never did get to ride in a helicopter, for instance."

"Maybe we can teach ourselves martial arts," I said. "If we put our heads together we can come up with our own form of fighting. We can call it Peter Drew Fu or something."

"Or Drew Peter Fu," Drew suggested.

"No offense, but that has a terrible ring to it," I said.

That weekend we invented our own form of martial arts. We realized we had to use our main strengths (namely, lack

119

of size and slightly-above-average speed) to our advantage. To be honest, it was pretty basic, consisting of only two moves:

Move #1. Shoving someone in the back before they have a chance to realize you're even there, followed by

Move #2. Running away.

We focused our training mostly on the second move, "land-skiing," all afternoon. Behind Drew's backyard is a thick forest full of evergreens that severely slopes all the way down to the main road. Land-skiing is this thing I came up with where you just start running as fast as you can down the steep hill, and because the ground is covered with slippery pine needles you eventually start gliding in your sneakers. I got the idea because of the way I'd flown down the stairs so fast after detention, escaping the Sweet brothers. The key to land-skiing is you have to jump to the side in order to weave around the trees, and we quickly became experts at weaving down the hill like this.

It's really fun (and incredibly dangerous).

On Monday it was time to test out what we'd learned. In the lobby before homeroom we saw the Sweet brothers in the corner, and they looked bigger than I'd remembered. The thought of actually trying to shove them didn't seem so bright an idea anymore. And we couldn't really use our land-skiing abilities, because the hallways were flat. "We could run away," Drew suggested. "We could start land-skiing right now, and by nightfall I bet we could hit the New Hampshire border."

Instead we thought outside the box and came up with an alternate solution, using the school's circular shape to our advantage: Basically, after every class I'd head to the left no matter what to get to my next class, even if the next class was closer by heading to the right. Then, if I spotted the Sweet brothers coming my way, I'd simply change directions, allowing me to avoid the Sweet brothers altogether. Drew used the same strategy.

It wasn't a perfect solution, though. The main problem was that it sometimes meant we had to do up to two laps around and we'd end up late for class (and really sweaty, too), but we figured it was worth not having to get bullied by the Sweet brothers. All day long we didn't run into them at all, thanks to our system.

Another good thing was that for the first time I noticed that we weren't the only kids being bullied by the Sweet brothers. It turned out just about everyone else was scared of them, too. Before English class I saw the Sweet brothers terrorize some seventh-grade girls from behind by shouting in their ears, and the two girls ran away, squealing. After math class I saw Carson get shoved into the lockers by Hank Sweet, and before social studies I was standing in the doorway and saw Trent changing directions right before he got to our class because the Sweet brothers were approaching him.

Apparently we weren't the only ones who had figured out this strategy.

fifteen

"**Y**OU KNOW, AT SOME POINT we're going to get unlucky and run right into them," Drew said on our walk home from school the next day.

"I know," I agreed. "Which is why we need to get going with the plan to trick everyone into thinking we're popular in every other town besides Fenwick."

We sat in Corbett Canyon making up our new identities: By day, we were the mysteriously isolated Peter and Drew, but outside of school we were the most popular kids in the neighboring town of Halliston. On weekends we went to birthday parties with all the cool kids at Halliston Middle and simply had no time to attend parties in Fenwick.

"But how can we prove we go to parties in Halliston?" I asked Drew.

"What about digital pictures?"

I put a hand on Drew's shoulder.

"There aren't actually any parties we're going to, remember?" I said real slowly.

"I know. I mean we could make fake pictures."

A good chill ran through me, as opposed to the bad kind you get right before you throw up.

"Drew, I have good news," I said. "You've officially gotten out of the box."

He beamed.

"Really?"

"You are box free, my friend," I said, and we high-fived. "Okay, so here's the deal. Tomorrow after school I'll borrow my dad's digital camera and we'll take a bunch of fake action shots of us hanging out at parties. What I need you to do is pick up some cheap party decorations so we can make the inside of the tree house look like someone's birthday party. Oh, and you need to order a birthday cake at Stop & Shop, which we'll pick up tomorrow. It should read, 'Happy Birthday, Emma!' because there aren't any Emmas in our grade."

"How much does a birthday cake cost?" Drew asked.

"Does it really matter?" I asked him.

"Kinda. I'm the one paying."

"You're wrong. There's no price to thinking outside the box."

"Okay, honestly I'm still not solid about this box thing."

"Forget the box! Just make sure you order the cake tonight. I have to go home for dinner. I'll bring the camera with me to school so we can come straight here afterward."

We shook on it.

All day long in classes the next day I was itching for school to be over so we could take our fake party pics. Students furiously scribbled notes as usual, but I couldn't concentrate. I would try to take notes for a minute, but my mind would wander. At the end of the day I ran into Sunny in the hall, and she asked me if I was ready to discuss my ideas in T.A.G. class.

"It's not until Wednesday," I corrected Sunny, patting her on the head. "You must be pretty high-strung these days, huh?"

"Today *is* Wednesday, genius," she said.

"Crap."

I took off to find Drew the second the bell rang. He was waiting for me by the entrance. "I forgot I have T.A.G. class now, I'll meet you at Corbett Canyon afterward."

I showed up late for class and already the room reeked of espresso, as Ms. Schoonmaker walked around the table. "As you're focusing on building your prototypes throughout the semester, you're also going to have to prepare your pitch describing the invention at the fair. So for today's class, let's go around and have you each describe one of your invention ideas to the class, and the rest of us will offer our two cents about it."

I glanced over at the cubbies on the shelves and groaned. Almost everyone had a big box or bag of some sort in it, along with pieces of wood, a hammer, an industrial-sized bottle of Elmer's glue, and a ruler. My cubby, of course, was empty. Sunny's yellow duffel bag was so full, it stuck halfway out of her cubby!

"Now, why don't you all take out a piece of paper and start listing the pros and cons of your invention, while I run down to the teachers' lounge for a refill," she said, waving her empty espresso cup (wafting the smelly fumes) as she left the room.

Everyone took out their notebooks. I was frazzled that I'd almost missed class, and that I seemed to be the only student who hadn't already started working on a prototype, but when I opened up my inventor's notebook I relaxed a little, remembering that I'd filled in a third of it with really good ideas.

When Ms. Schoonmaker returned, Carson started describing his idea—a calculator holder on his belt buckle, which we all quickly shot down because he'd be the only one to use it. "But more people would want to buy calculators if they had a place to wear it," he said in defense.

"That might be what some call a niche product—meaning, it's for a very specific consumer. We want to think broader," Ms. Schoonmaker said.

The good news is Sunny's idea didn't seem that promising, either. Her idea was to have glass pots for plants, so you could see the roots and stuff, like an ant farm. And there'd be a thermometer on the side of the pot, to tell you the temperature of the soil.

"Then if a plant wasn't doing well, we'd know it's because the soil's too cold," Sunny said. "Or if the soil's too dry, or overwatered."

"Very interesting," Ms. Schoonmaker said.

"Unfortunately it's still a niche product, just like Carson's calculator holster. Only plants that can afford health care would be able to buy it," I said. Everyone stared at me. "That sounded funnier in my head."

"Peter's right, though," Graham countered. "An ant farm is cool because you get to watch them build societies and stuff. A plant's roots, on the other hand, would barely move. It would be boring to watch."

Sunny's cheeks looked like they were boiling.

"It often takes several attempts before you hit on the right invention, or even perfect a promising one. It took Thomas Edison a thousand tries before he got the lightbulb to work, and he never thought of them as failures. I believe he said something to the effect that the lightbulb was an invention with a thousand steps," Ms. Schoonmaker said. She looked at me. "How about you, Peter?"

"So, let's see—so many ideas to choose from, oh, here's one. I have an idea for something I call the Urban Sound Machine. It's for city people like Carson."

"City people?" he said.

"Remember when you moved here from New York and you hated how quiet it was?" I asked Carson, and he nodded suspiciously. "Well, this would be a sound machine to help city people sleep when they're in quieter areas. For example, there would be a setting on the dial that makes it sound like a construction worker's outside your window, working a drill all night long."

"Have you ever even been to a city?" Carson asked me.

I ignored him and described the other settings, but everyone frowned.

"The home-invasion sound would give older people heart attacks," Sunny said.

"No, it wouldn't—it's the quiet that city people hate, isn't that true, Carson?"

"Let's bring it down a notch, Peter," Ms. Schoonmaker said.

"That was just when I first moved here," Carson said.

"Now when I visit my uncle in the Bronx, I can't stand how loud it is."

Sunny pretended to look really thoughtful by twisting her mouth and tapping the table with her pencil. "Maybe this is more of a gag gift, Peter?"

"It's not a gag gift!" I shouted.

The late bell rang.

"Look!" I said, pointing at Carson. "Everyone jumped a little in their seats when the bell rang except him."

Ms. Schoonmaker put down her mini cup of espresso.

"Peter, what did I say about shouting in class? Okay, good session, everybody, being able to really think about and critique each other's inventions helps develop the creative mind. For next time, I want you to write a one-page description of the invention you want to focus on this semester, and try to think ahead of time about why people would possibly say no to it."

Sunny was smiling at me as we left the library.

"Urban sound machine?" she said. "What were you thinking?"

"Hey, look," I said, pointing at the spider plant in the corner. "I think that leaf just moved . . . how fascinating."

It was starting to get dark when I got outside, and we hadn't even taken our fake party pics yet! I booked it all the way to Drew's house, climbed up to the tree house, and groaned. He hadn't decorated the inside so it would resemble a real party, like I'd instructed him.

"What the heck have you been doing all afternoon?" I asked.

"I ate a snack inside," he said, and I scowled at him. "What? That takes time."

"Where's the cake?"

"I was waiting for you."

"Drew, it's getting dark out!"

"Wouldn't the party be at night?"

"I guess you're right. Come on, let's go get it and then set things up."

I had to borrow his dad's old ten-speed, but the seat was so high that I could barely pedal, so I ended up sort of rowing with my legs. We finally got to Stop & Shop and picked up the birthday cake. When I saw it, I started feeling better—it was perfect! It read in cursive, "Happy Birthday, Emma!" across the top with blue icing. Drew had five bucks left over, so we visited the florist next to the bakery and bought a red rose to add to the fake decorations. We discovered that the premade bouquets had this wet green foamy square inside the pots that the flowers stuck out of, and it felt neat to poke our fingers into them. But then the florist yelled at us for ruining the bouquets and we took off before she could arrest us.

We biked back, and Drew got some birthday candles in his kitchen. We took it up to the tree house, then set up a tiny table to go with our two beach chairs inside. We positioned ourselves around the lit candles and put on big smiles as if we were having a great time watching the imaginary Emma blow out her candles. It took some practice, but we figured out eventually how to shoot it so it looked like we were at a huge party. Drew would wear a long-sleeve shirt so his elbow would be in the corner of the picture, and I'd be next to him. Then he'd change his outfit so it would look like I was standing next to someone else in the next pic.

I even convinced Drew to put on a few of Mrs. N's dresses to impersonate actual girls at the party—I made sure to only include Drew's shoulder in the shot so it looked like I was standing next to a hot girl, or at least a girl with a really hot arm. When we were done, we looked through the photos, and I had to admit they looked pretty authentic.

"Do you really think this will work?" Drew asked.

"There's nothing like cold, hard proof to convince everyone we're cool," I said.

On Thursday morning Drew and I took out the camera in homeroom and started looking at the pics. I fake-laughed really loudly to get everyone's attention. As I'd hoped, everyone huddled around us to see what we were looking at. The plan was working!

"Oh man, that one's so embarrassing," I said, staring at a picture of me with a big mouthful of cake, giving the photographer two thumbs-ups—a girl in a strapless red dress had her left arm draped over my shoulders.

"What are those pictures of?" Shawn asked.

"Oh, our friend Emma's birthday was on Saturday, we had no choice but to go to Emma's because she went to our birthday parties this summer, and anyway I forgot until this morning that her mom's camera was broken, so I'd let her use mine," I explained.

"Where was the party? Why's everything made out of wood?" he asked.

Shawn was right. I looked at the pictures for the first time as if I was someone else, and it really did look like they were taken inside a tree house.

"Her parents are crazy about wood paneling," Drew said.

"That's Emma," I said, pointing to another picture of me standing next to Drew's shoulder, when he was wearing his mom's yellow dress. I silently prayed nobody would recognize the remarkably Texas-shaped mole on his shoulder, but otherwise Drew was so scrawny that he did make for a pretty good imitation of a girl's shoulder.

"These are action shots of when Emma blew out the

candles," I explained. "I'm laughing so hard because they were trick candles and kept relighting. It was funny because she has pretty bad asthma and was starting to hyperventilate or something."

"Why did her mom take all these pictures of just Peter? Why wouldn't she take pictures of her own daughter blowing out the candles?"

"Um, we're family friends, we go to Maine together for a week every summer," I said. Luckily, the bell rang and I quickly turned the camera off. "Okeydokey, time to put the party shots away."

Everyone looked really confused. Drew sighed.

"Okay, everyone, quiet down, I have an announcement to make," Mr. Davis said. "It seems a fair number of students have lost personal items since school started, and Principal Curtis has instructed us to remind you to keep better track of your belongings. Make a mental check before you leave each class to make sure you haven't left anything on your desks, that sort of thing."

"Wait a sec—where's my hat?" Shawn asked, acting really panicked.

"It's on your head," Sally said.

Shawn felt his head and sighed really loudly. Then he got that panicked look in his face again.

"Wait a sec—where's my shoes?"

Everyone laughed.

"Okay, knock it off," Mr. Davis said, but even he was smiling.

Drew poked me in the ribs.

"You should be the one coming up with hilarious jokes like that," he scolded me.

"I know," I said sadly.

At the beginning of each class that morning, I showed the pics to more classmates, and the results were mixed at best. They weren't nearly as impressed as I thought they would be, but on the other hand, not a single student accused me of faking the party pics, and I figured that was better than nothing. Plus, there was an added bonus. In English class I was feeling guilty that everyone was taking notes the whole time, but then when the bell rang, Heidi suddenly realized her mechanical pencil was missing, and I think Mr. Vensel was just as bored as everyone else, because he immediately got down on his hands and knees to help her look for it. Anyway, it was this moment when it dawned on me that I could simply take secret pictures of the chalkboard instead of having to take notes! My idea was that the night before a test or something I'd simply zoom the pictures on my dad's computer and study the photographs until I learned everything. Maybe this thinking-outside-the-box thing hadn't changed our lives just yet, but it certainly had its benefits.

* * *

On Friday I continued to secretly take digital pictures of the blackboard in my classes while my classmates feverishly took notes, and then spent the rest of the time writing in my inventor's notebook. At lunchtime Principal Curtis showed up and motioned for everyone to quiet down. "Listen up, everybody," he said. "The Lost-and-Found Forum on the school website is absolutely stuffed, and after interviewing several of the students who have lost items in the last few weeks, we've come to the conclusion that either there is a thief in this school or stealing in general has risen abnormally this fall."

The students started murmuring nervously.

"Now, there's no need for panic, but you really have to be diligent—not only about watching your own things, but also about keeping an eye out for suspicious activity. If you see anything suspicious, just tell a teacher or visit me at my office. That is all, for now. Enjoy the rest of your lunches."

Principal Curtis exited the cafeteria, and everyone started chattering real loudly.

"I can't believe this is happening," Drew said.

Surprisingly, some students didn't believe there really was a thief. Mrs. Farley, who had lunch-monitor duty that day, suggested to Carson at the next table over that there was no thief. "I've been teaching for twenty years, and the one thing middle schoolers have in common is that they all lose personal possessions constantly. It's just a bigger deal nowadays because they have more expensive things to lose."

It seemed weird to me that everyone was so freaked out about this thief business. Me and Drew, we had worse things to worry about. These people had such easy lives, to worry about this thief when me and Drew were barely hanging on.

As the days passed, more students' things went missing:

Angie's favorite bracelet.

Carson's scientific calculator.

An eighth grader's wallet.

Sally's horseshoe key chain.

A seventh grader's earbuds.

It became a daily occurrence where in at least one of my classes someone would find out that they were missing something: a hoodie, a cell phone, a T-shirt, a textbook. In fact, Drew and I at one point realized that we were the only kids who hadn't gotten anything stolen, it seemed.

"Even the thief doesn't include us," Drew said, and I nodded sadly.

Unluckily for us, our wish was granted, because when I went to my locker at the end of the day to get Drew's jacket, it was gone! Drew showed up a moment later, and I gritted my teeth. "Um, I have some not-so-great news that kind of involves you," I said. "Your jacket's missing."

"You lost my jacket?"

"Not necessarily, the thief might've stolen it," I said.

"But you have a history of losing your jacket, so maybe the thief has nothing to do with it."

"Either way I'm in the clear, right?"

"How so?"

"If the thief stole it, that's not my fault," I said. "And if I really did lose your jacket, well, you already knew about this tendency of mine beforehand. So really, to be fair, in a way it's more your fault that you let me borrow it in the first place, because now I feel bad for losing it and it's not like I could help it."

"That's not a good excuse."

I shrugged my shoulders.

"We're different people," I said. "I guess I'm just the type of kid who, when I put a quarter in the claw machine at the arcade and fail to pick up a toy, I don't get angry because I know there was always that risk that I wouldn't succeed."

"I guess you're right."

He didn't say anything else, and this kinda annoyed me—I wanted to point out that if he was a bigger man he'd apologize for putting me in this situation in the first place, but this was one of those rare moments in life where I knew to quit while I was ahead. Then I thought of something.

"Hey—what if it *was* the thief?" I asked.

For the first time we really considered this possibility, and it gave us the chills.

By the end of the following week, more students had stuff go missing. Everyone was talking about it, because in any group of friends in any grade, at least one person had lost something at school, and there was no doubt about it at this point—there was definitely a thief at the school.

sixteen

Mrs. Ryder handed back our first pop quizzes in math class on Monday.

"To give you an idea of where you stand in class, the average score was 81 percent. That's not very high. It means some of you aren't paying enough attention. If you have questions, don't be afraid to ask. If you scored below a 65 percent, you received an F, which means you have to get your quiz signed by your parents tonight."

I looked around to see who got F's, but nobody frowned or groaned when they got their quiz back. Either everyone had really good poker faces or Mrs. Ryder was exaggerating about the bad grades. She finally dropped off my quiz and patted it on the desk. "Make sure you get this back to me tomorrow," she said out loud, and everyone in class went,

"Oooooh!"

I looked down at the quiz, and on top it read:

14%. F–

An F–? I didn't even know that was possible. A 14 percent? How could I have scored so low? After class I pleaded my case with her. "I'll show my parents the quiz, but do they really have to sign it?" I asked. "They hate signing stuff. They're paranoid about having their identities stolen. We have an uncle who lost it all because he talked to a telemarketer one day. Now he's in a shelter, eating unlabeled cans of soup."

"You also have to answer all the questions again, on a separate piece of paper."

"You're giving me more homework?" I asked, although technically I hadn't done any of it all semester, but still.

That night I couldn't eat during dinner. Mom had made chicken potpie, which I can't stand to begin with, because the fact is, pies should always be filled with dessert. I do like the square-shaped carrots, though, because the shape makes them feel futuristic. I can't wait for the day when we just eat pills instead of food, but I'm getting off topic, and I have a feeling I wouldn't even think this way if I had a mother who could actually cook. The point is, my stomach was in knots, and I ended up nibbling on a couple of soupy square carrots.

"You have to eat more than that," Dad said. "Your mom spent a long time defrosting this meal."

Sunny ate heartily. She could afford to, since she had all A's.

"By the way, I have something you have to sign later," I said real casually.

"What is it?" he asked.

"Oh—nothing important, just something for math class."

"Are you going on a field trip?"

"Maybe, I don't even know, you just have to give me your signature on some silly piece of paper, it's nothing, really. Just let me know next time you're signing bills and checks, and I'll have you add your John Hancock to it. No biggy."

"Nonsense, go run upstairs and get it."

I exhaled softly. I trudged up to my room and took out my math folder. I turned the quiz upside down and slid the bottom of it out of the folder so you could only see blank white space. I went back downstairs.

"Okay, sign here," I said.

"What is it? Let me see," Dad said.

"He's hiding something," Sunny said. "Make him show you the whole page."

"Believe you me, it's just not worth your time," I said,

giving Sunny the evil eye. "I'm trying to save you from boredom. Just sign it, okay?"

Everyone stared at me. I sighed, and slid the folder over to my parents.

Dad took out the quiz and Mom cried, "Fourteen percent?"

Sunny's eyes got big. She scooted out of her seat and stood over Mom.

"You only answered one out of ten questions right," Sunny said, and her forehead crinkled. "That means she gave you four bonus points for writing your name correctly."

"How did you do so terribly on this quiz?" Dad asked.

"Well, for one thing, it was a pop quiz."

"You just added and subtracted the numbers!" Sunny laughed.

"I know." I jumped on this factoid. "So shouldn't I have gotten half credit on all the answers, then?"

"How are we possibly related?" she replied, staring at me.

"Sunny, you're going to have to teach your brother how to do this kind of math. I have to finish up some work tonight," Dad said.

"I don't have time for this!" she cried.

"And I don't need her help!" I said.

"Yes, you do," he replied.

"But it never works," I complained. "You tried to get her

to help me practice the recorder, remember?"

"Sunny said you refused to practice," Mom pointed out.

"Exactly, some teacher, huh?" I replied. It suddenly dawned on me for the first time that maybe I intentionally didn't practice the recorder because I didn't want Sunny to ever be praised for rescuing me. I didn't mention this to them, though, because it would only get me in more trouble.

Dad turned to Sunny.

"Sit with your brother and teach him what he did wrong. I'll sign this once you figure out all the right answers."

"This isn't fair!" Sunny groaned. "Why can't you just accept that he's hopeless? It'll make life easier for the rest of us."

"You're referring to yourself as 'us,' which is plural," I said, winking at my dad. "See, I'm more of an English guy than a math guy, really."

He stared at me like I was an alien with a solid grasp of the English language.

"No arguing," he said. "That's final."

After dinner I had to sit with Sunny in the dining room, and she tried to teach me how to do the math.

"So what do you actually know?" she asked.

I took out a piece of paper and wrote my name in big letters:

PETER

"That's not funny," she said.

"I don't consider four points a laughing matter, either," I replied.

She sighed, and pointed at the parentheses in the first problem. "What are these?"

"It means the numbers inside are secret?"

She rolled her eyes.

"Do you pay any attention in class?"

"I'm not being serious," I pointed out to her.

"That's exactly your problem, you don't take it seriously, and that's why you're failing."

"But I'm never going to use this math in real life, so what difference does it make?"

"It doesn't matter. If you don't do well, you won't get into college."

"That's in, like, thirty years, and I'll be a millionaire by the time I graduate high school because of my inventions."

"Thirty years?" she gaped at me. "You can't even do basic addition!"

"Again, I think you're not getting my humor," I said.

"You don't get it. Plus, you'll get kicked out of the T.A.G. program if you don't maintain at least a B average."

"That's ridiculous, what do my grades have to do with inventing?"

"It's called The Academically Gifted program, you idiot! Of course your grades matter," she said. My stomach fell.

"You don't belong in there, anyway."

"Ms. Schoonmaker would never allow it," I said softly, but I had a sinking feeling Sunny was right. "It's not fair, you're the one who thought the oval looked like a spider!"

"How's it going in here?" Mom asked, entering the room.

"He's hopeless, can I go now?" Sunny asked.

"Not until he figures it out."

"But that'll take forever!" Sunny cried. Mom just ignored her and went back into the living room. My sister and I resumed glaring at each other.

"Look," I finally said. "We both want to get out of here, and the only way is if you answer the questions correctly for me and say I learned it."

She considered it for a couple of seconds.

"Fine," she replied, and started filling in the answers.

I watched her race through the quiz. She kept shaking her head and rolling her eyes to show how easy it was for her, and I started daydreaming about one day having to tutor her for something and making a big fuss out of how dumb she was, just so she could see how lame it is for someone to do that. But then she'd probably point out that if I was the bigger man, I wouldn't have stooped to her level in the first place, in which case I'd have to explain that—

"It's really creepy when you just sit there with your mouth open, staring into space," she said. "Now come on, just copy it over in your handwriting and we can be done here."

I started copying her answers onto a fresh piece of paper, but then I got the feeling she was sabotaging me or something. "Are you sure these are all right?" I eyed her suspiciously.

"Most of them."

"That's what I thought! Come on, they *all* have to be right."

"Mrs. Ryder would never buy that you could go from getting a zero to a perfect score just like that. It has to be realistic."

"Actually, it was a fourteen percent, remember?" I corrected her.

She rolled her eyes.

"Just hurry up and finish copying the answers, I have homework to do."

When I was finished, I showed it to Dad, and he finally signed the quiz.

"I don't want to see another one of these again," he said.

"I tried not to show you in the first place," I said.

"This isn't a joke."

"I wasn't joking."

"Oh, Peter," he said, and took off his reading glasses and started rubbing his eyes.

By the time he opened them, I was long gone. I went

back to my room to call Drew, and told him what Sunny had said. "She's lying, right?"

"Your sister wouldn't lie," he said. "You're going to have to pull up your grade in math class."

"It's too late, I'm too far behind because I haven't been paying attention in class. What we need to do is make an amazing prototype for the invention contest."

Drew sighed into the phone.

"I thought we were focusing on making people believe we're popular in other towns?" he asked.

"This is way easier, because I already know I'm the best inventor. We need to focus on the inventions contest. They wouldn't kick out the star of the class, right?"

"I guess not," Drew said, but he didn't sound nearly as excited about my new plan as I figured he'd be.

Seventeen

I MET UP WITH DREW AT Corbett Canyon after school the next day, and we tried to figure out which invention to make a prototype for. The mini cats idea, unfortunately, was still in "development stage," according to Ms. Schoonmaker. The Mr. Home Security was a no-go, too; I felt like I needed to be an electrician to even begin to know how to rig that up. And the Urban Sound Machine idea had already gotten shot down. I whimpered. Even though I had three-quarters of my inventor's notebook filled, I didn't have a single idea I could possibly take to the prototype stage!

"Maybe we could tape-record construction sounds and glass breaking, and play it during the competition to see if Carson conks out?" Drew suggested.

"He'll just force himself to stay awake," I replied,

feverishly flipping through the pages. "I guess that leaves the self-lighting cigarette."

"I don't know about that one—smoking's really bad for you."

"I can't get smokers to stop smoking, but at least I can get them to stop killing so many trees and wasting so much precious fuel lighting them," I said, but he frowned. "I don't have a choice—it's my only doable idea!"

"I don't know . . . ," Drew said. "Besides, you can't make a prototype of that without the real thing."

"Huh?"

"You'd need cigarettes to make a prototype, right?"

He was right. Great, I thought, another wrinkle.

Since none of our parents smoked, we biked over to the 7-Eleven. We spotted a high-school kid smoking a cigarette in the parking lot by the green Dumpster.

"Jackpot!" I said to Drew, and we rolled up to him. "Hey, guy, could you buy me a pack of cigarettes? I have money."

"Smoking's bad for you!" the high schooler said.

At first I thought it was kinda touching how this older kid was looking out for my general health like this, but then I realized he was lying a second later when he took out a pack of gum and Drew asked him for a piece.

"Sorry, dude, gum's bad for you," he muttered, then walked away.

"It was sugar-free gum, though," Drew said sadly to nobody in particular.

"I guess we're going to have to buy cigarettes on our own," I said. "But I don't look even close to eighteen."

"You don't even look like you're twelve," Drew said.

"You're only four pounds heavier than me!" I shouted.

"Hey, I didn't say I looked any older."

I sighed.

"Well, those four pounds don't lie. I guess you just have to go in and see if they'll sell cigarettes to you, and then we take it from there," I said.

"No way, it's your invention!"

"But we're partners, Drew."

He pursed his lips and shook his head. My legs started shaking, as if I was at a sleepover at Drew's house and we'd just run out of candy. We parked our bikes by the air pumps in the back in case we needed a quick getaway. I was tempted to pop some quarters into the air pumps so I could blow mulch all over the place for fun, but I forced myself to focus on the mission. I took out the emergency twenty-dollar bill that my parents make me keep in my wallet in case I ever get abducted and manage to escape and need to catch a bus home or something.

I pulled open the glass door and headed inside. As I entered the store, there was a fake bell sound and I winced.

The cashier, a middle-aged woman reading a newspaper, looked over at me and nodded before returning to her reading. This gave me a little confidence—I figured maybe she'd be so into whatever she was reading that she wouldn't even notice that I was actually twelve. I went up to the counter. Then I had to back up a step so she could see me. I cleared my throat.

"Can I help you?" she said, not looking away from her paper. Excellent!

"Oh—hey there, I just got off work," I said, fake-yawning. "Uh, I just need a pack of smokes and a lottery ticket. Wait, scratch that, I forgot, the city doesn't pay me till Thursday, just get me the smokes and I'll come back tomorrow for the lottery ticket."

She finally looked at me. Her eyes were half-lidded, which didn't look promising; it's the same expression Fluffy gives me right before she tries to claw my eyes out.

"How old are you?" she asked.

I tried to smile at her in a flirty way, but I probably looked like I was having a double hernia or something.

"How old do you want me to be?" I replied, because that's something I heard a lady say to a guy in an R-rated movie once, only in the movie the lady's voice didn't crack when she said it. I think they were both drunk, and even though I didn't see the end of it, I'm pretty sure the guy shot the lady at the end.

"Do you want me to call the police or your parents?" she asked, picking up the phone, and I sprinted out of the store to the air pumps, where Drew was waiting. He must have guessed it was going to go badly, because he was already on his bike, holding mine up next to him as if we were riding horses in an old Western. We peeled out of the parking lot and didn't stop until we got back to Corbett Canyon. For the first time, I looked behind us, positive that police cars would be chasing us, but the road was empty.

"Back to the drawing board," Drew sighed.

"That was stressful. I could really use a cigarette right about now," I said, and Drew slapped me! "I was kidding."

"Don't kid. Smoking's bad for you. Maybe this is good, we shouldn't be messing with those things."

"You just aren't seeing the big picture, Drew."

"Well, at least I'm no longer in that box."

"Oh brother," I said.

That night during study hours I sat there thinking about my idea for self-lighting cigarettes. Drew was right, how could I possibly make a prototype if I didn't actually have any cigarettes to work with? I was completely stuck, but the next day at school I had a stroke of luck in science class—we were burning chemicals over a Bunsen burner to record the reactions. The chemicals lit up in different colors when you held them over the flame. Mr. Reardon picked out random partners for lab, and I ended up working with Angie! I figured I'd impress her somehow and maybe that would get me on the invite list for her next party. I started burning chemicals and she seemed impressed.

"You know, this would make for a really cool display at, say, a social event, um . . . on the weekend," I suggested.

"I have no idea what you're talking about," she said.

I sighed. She started recording results in her lab notebook, but all was not lost, because for once I actually enjoyed science class. I just mindlessly burned stuff over the Bunsen burners for a few minutes until Angie started complaining.

"You're wasting the phosphorous, we need more of it," she said. "Come on, we have to burn seven more chemicals before class is over."

"But I like the yellow color this one makes," I said.

Mr. Reardon stopped by our station.

"Do you know what phosphorous is used for?" he asked.

"Nope," I said, scorching another piece over the Bunsen burner.

"It's used in making matches."

"That's really interesting," I said, not really paying attention at first, but then a second later something clicked. "Wait—what?"

"Basically when combined with friction, it causes the flame to spark on the tip of a match," he explained.

That was it! The key to my prototype was to simply glue some phosphorous to the end of a cigarette, then you could just rub the tip of it against a matchbook surface. I could get hold of an empty cigarette pack and glue the striking surface of a matchbook onto the side. Then I could just make a substitute cigarette by finding something roughly the same size and shape as a real one, and glue phosphorous to the tip. That would be my self-lighting cigarette for the competition!

Which meant that I was going to have to steal some phosphorous from the class in order to build my prototype. I'd never stolen anything before. But it wasn't really stealing, I reasoned, because I was planning on returning the vial when I was done. Besides, if I got busted, I could just say I did it in the name of science, and who would appreciate that more than a science teacher?

The period was almost over, and Mr. Reardon returned to his desk. I waited for Angie to start talking to Heidi sitting next to her, and then when the coast seemed clear, I casually grabbed two vials of chemicals and slipped them into my pocket. The bell rang. Mr. Reardon announced the homework assignment, and then we all poured out the door.

When I got home, I found some matches in the living room, grabbed a spoon from the kitchen, then ran up to my room and shut the door. I opened up the vial of phosphorous. I even put on an old pair of sunglasses for protection, just like in science class. All I had to do was glue some phosphorous to the end of the eraser, but since I'm addicted to fireworks, I really wanted to light up the crystals and see that bright yellow color one more time before working on the prototype.

The phosphorous crystals were like chunks of rock salt, and I tapped out a spoonful into my hand. I smelled them. I licked them. They tasted salty. Very interesting. I jiggled most of them back into the vial; some fell onto the carpet. I took a single crystal and placed it on the spoon. Usually in lab we'd use metal pincers to pick up a single crystal and hold it over the Bunsen flame. I carefully lifted up the spoon, lit a match with my other hand and held the flame under the spoon. Five seconds passed. Ten. I knew it would take longer because I had to first heat up the spoon, but the match went out. I lit another, and stared at the crystal like it was a kernel of popping corn. The match burned down to the nub and singed my fingers. Why wasn't this working? Maybe I needed to light more than one crystal at once. I sprinkled more phosphorous onto the spoon, but it still wouldn't light up like it had in science class.

"It smells like matches," Sunny said, coming into my room.

"Get out of my room, you know the rules," I said without looking up.

"There's no rule that I can't enter your room! What are you doing?"

"I'm working on my prototype for T.A.G. class."

"Are those chemicals from the science lab?"

"I have special permission, because I got to class late and he said to do it at home," I lied. "I think these chemicals are defective, anyhow."

"You moron, a match won't produce nearly enough heat to ignite them."

I really have to pay more attention in school, I thought.

"Did you steal those from the lab?" she asked.

"I said I'm only borrowing them for an experiment. I'm going to return them tomorrow."

Eventually she left. I kept messing around with the chemicals, and when I heard the garage door open ten minutes later, I placed everything in my desk drawer and closed it. A minute later my mom came charging into the room with Sunny right behind her.

"What are you doing in here? Sunny says you're burning chemicals?"

"I'm testing out stuff for inventor's class, but no, I didn't actually succeed in burning chemicals, so you can relax," I said.

"It's for a school experiment?"

I wanted to say yes, but I couldn't lie to my mom's face.

"I'm returning them tomorrow," I said quietly, which was the truth.

"I'm calling your science teacher to see why I never heard about this before. It seems dangerous," Mom said, leaving the room.

Sunny shook her head at me.

"How's it going, narc?" I asked her.

"I'm hall monitor," she said. "I have an obligation to report this."

"We're nowhere near a hall!" I shouted. "You're just afraid my invention will beat yours."

"I don't think I have to worry about someone who actually thought he could burn up chemicals with a measly match," she said, and left the room.

She had a point there.

When my dad got home from work and found out what I'd done, he was even madder than my mom.

"Why did you steal the chemicals?" he asked.

"It was for . . . I d'no," my voice trailed off because I knew he wouldn't understand, anyway.

"I'm very disappointed in you, Peter. You know not to

steal. Did you ever stop to think about what your actions might lead to?"

I shrugged.

"Well, you're going to have plenty of time to think about it in detention."

My stomach felt like it had vaulted into my throat. For the record, stomachs taste really gross. "What?" I asked.

"Your mother just got off the phone with your science teacher, and he said you were lying about borrowing the chemicals, and he's given you detention every day for a month, starting after school on Friday," he said, and my stomach fell into my left sock. "You should be grateful you didn't get in more trouble than that."

For the record, it's hard to feel grateful when your stomach's squishing around in your left sock.

I told Drew about my death sentence on the walk to school the next morning. He didn't know how to console me, so we just walked in silence. Every now and then he'd pat me on the shoulder and smile weakly at me, but it was like he was staring at a ghost.

I looked for Ms. Schoonmaker before homeroom, figuring maybe she could get me out of detention. I found her in the teachers' lounge, standing over her espresso machine in the corner, carefully brewing a fresh cup. I explained the situation as she stood there stinking up the place with her drink. Finally she put her cup down and said, "You are aware that there's a thief in our school—do you realize how this looks?"

"I'm not the thief!"

"Why did you steal the chemicals, Peter?" she asked.

I sighed.

"Everyone keeps using that word," I said. "I wasn't stealing, I was only borrowing them for your class. I was working on a prototype for my invention."

"What is it?"

"Self-lighting cigarettes," I said, and she frowned. "Don't worry, I'm not using real cigarettes. I was going to glue phosphorus, the stuff matches are made of, onto the eraser tip of a pencil, as if it was a cigarette, and there'd be a match strike strip on the side of the cigarette box."

"Let me get this straight—your goal is to make smoking easier for people?"

"It's an environmental invention! It would save countless trees, and gas, by eliminating matchbooks and lighters."

"Smoking's a deadly habit, I can't condone you trying to make it easier."

"Can you just ignore the fact that it's a deadly habit for just one minute and see the creativity behind it? I need you to think outside the box on this one."

"It's a clever idea, I suppose, but self-lighting cigarettes would ultimately make the world a more unhealthy place to live in, which defeats the purpose of the project. I'm sorry, Peter, but you're going to have to come up with something else."

"Fine, but can you get me out of detention now that you know it was for one of my classes? I'm supposed to have detention every day after school."

"You still took the chemicals without even trying to get permission."

"I didn't ask only because I knew he'd say no," I said softly.

She exhaled, and it took a huge amount of willpower to not grimace. I made a mental note to brainstorm later an invention that would eliminate coffee breath. I wanted to tell her my idea to prove how my inventor's mind was always running, but teachers are the worst people in the world at accepting constructive criticism.

"Rules are rules, and they can't be bent. You're going to have to miss some T.A.G. classes, it seems."

"Oh, okay, so we're not quite on the same page," I explained. "I was thinking actually more along the lines of you getting me out of detention altogether."

"Go to homeroom, Peter," she said.

I tried to explain that T.A.G. was the only class I even liked, but she shooed me out, filling the room with her espresso breath with all the shooing, so I had no choice but to leave. Sunny was in the hallway, and she looked weird. That is, she always looked upset—that's how intense she was about school, but this time I noticed she had a creepy smile plastered on her face. "What's with you?" I asked.

Her smile faded.

"What?" she snapped.

"You had a big creepy smile on your face just now."

"So?"

"Were you spying on my meeting with Ms. Schoon-maker?"

"As if I even care what happens to you," she scoffed, and then stomped off.

eighteen

I WAS HOPING IT WOULD BE one of those crummy Fridays that seem to last forever, but unfortunately the day passed really quickly. What a waste, usually I really enjoy weirdly fast days, but this time it was sheer torture because my body felt like it was falling down a dark hole the entire time. Before I knew it, the bell rang, and everyone left the building except me. I made the slow walk over to room 12. It didn't seem fair. Drew and I had successfully avoided the Sweet brothers all this time, and now I had been thrown to the wolves by someone in my own family.

Drew appeared in my brain as I touched the doorknob. *You need to run away right now*, he warned me. *Land-ski to New Hampshire. By nightfall you could make it!* I silently reminded Drew that this was impossible, and then prayed that by some miracle the Sweet brothers had turned overnight into good, law-abiding citizens and had gotten out of detention, but of course they were sitting in the front row. Apparently detention is the one thing they're always on time for in school. They were intensely drawing pictures and at first they didn't notice me, and I was tempted to slowly back away and just skip detention and hopefully get it changed to an at-home suspension or something, but then they looked up at me and I froze.

"You again?" Hugh said. "Sunny Lee's goody-goody brother managed to get another detention? I don't believe it."

"I have it every day for a month," I admitted, hoping it would make them feel less urgent about mauling me afterward.

The Sweet brothers looked shocked. And to my astonishment, they just nodded disinterestedly, then returned to drawing pictures of surprisingly realistic monsters. I handed my detention slip to Mr. Tinsley, who stuck it in a folder without even looking up at me. Hank waved me over with a strange smile on his face, and I sat down next to him cautiously, ready to up and run the moment he tried to attack me, but instead he started talking to me as if he had no recollection whatsoever of the previous month of child abuse they'd been doling out on me and Drew.

"So what are you in for?" Hank asked.

Was this a trick question? This was a pop test! What was the right answer? I had to impress him. I racked my brain for exciting answers. Defacing school property? Assault with a deadly weapon? Espionage?

"You don't want to know," I said eventually.

They considered this for a moment.

"I guess you really aren't like Sunny," Hugh finally said. "She'd never get detention."

"I told you I'm not like her."

"Street Magic's crazy!" Hank said.

"Actually, I'm Street Magic's Assistant," I clarified, then cringed, expecting them to be mad at me. But instead they chuckled!

"If I draw you a maze, will you do me a favor and try to solve it?" Hugh asked me. I gaped at him. "I'm serious—give me five minutes, I bet you won't be able to solve it."

What the heck was going on? I placed my book bag on the floor next to my desk. A minute passed. Then another. Just the sound of Hugh's pencil. Mr. Tinsley was sitting at his desk, grading papers and listening to classical music on his headphones. I glanced under the desk to make sure there wasn't an M-80 fizzing away under the seat. There wasn't. A minute later, Hugh put his notebook on my desk and giggled quietly as I intentionally screwed up, running my pencil into dead ends, because I thought it was another trap and that he'd beat me up if I solved it too quickly.

"You're not very good at mazes," Hugh said.

"Actually, I am, you're just good at making them," I replied.

"Really?" he asked. I nodded. "Thanks, Street Magic's Assis—er, Peter."

And then he smiled at me! I'd never seen either of the Sweet brothers smile like this before. This *had* to be a trick, or probably they just had no choice but to be nice to me while a teacher sat ten feet away. I pictured the darkened hallway and it made my belly ache. While it was embarrassing to get bullied in front of everyone during school, I realized now that it was better to get bullied in public because that meant there were witnesses. The janitor was vacuuming a few classrooms away. I prayed he'd be out in the hallway at the end of detention to protect me, even though ever since I'd punched him in the face after the straitjacket incident he seemed to kind of hate me.

The late bell rang.

"Well, it's been real," I said, slowly standing up. Hugh and Hank were whispering to each other and my heart sank— they were plotting how best to attack me. I got as far as the door before Hugh called out to me.

"Hey, Peter, do you want to hit the mall with us?" he asked.

"The mall? Why?"

Hugh almost looked shy when I said this, and I was sure he was just acting.

"I dunno, um, we could hang out is all, you don't have to if you don't want to, nobody's forcing you. I just figured since it's now the weekend, you could hang out."

Or was he?

"Okay," I said. "But how are we going to get there?"

"You can ride on my handlebars," he offered.

It was nice of Hugh to pedal both of us all the way to the mall like that, but at the same time it was easily the single most terrifying ride of my life. We rode in the direction of oncoming traffic on the left side, and as strong as Hugh was, he wavered over the white line a bunch of times struggling to pedal both of us as I sat like an imprisoned bird on his front handlebars with my feet draped over the front wheel. At any moment he could have slammed on his brakes, even by accident, and I would have pitched forward and splattered all over a passing windshield. Hugh must have heard me moaning the whole time, because at one point he shouted, "Don't worry, me and Hank share bikes all the time and it's totally safe," and he patted me on the shoulder reassuringly. But when he took one hand off the handlebars, the bike swerved inward toward a truck, and I almost had a heart attack. "Whoops, my bad," he laughed nervously.

We finally made it to the mall in one piece, and I followed them over to Lids, a baseball-cap store, to try on dozens. I never wear baseball caps (thanks to my mom pounding the fact into my brain for years that you lose your hair if you wear them regularly), but the Sweet brothers wanted me to try on a bunch of different caps, and I pretended to be really into it.

"That one looks pretty good on you," Hugh said, stuffing a brown Padres cap onto my head. "You should buy it."

"I definitely would if I had any dough," I replied. "It feels so good on my . . . head."

"Why don't you have any money?" Hank asked me.

"Um, because I'm twelve?"

"No worries," Hugh said, massaging my shoulders from behind incredibly hard, the way my uncle does at family reunions. I gritted my teeth and pretended it didn't kill. "You can get it another time."

"Well, that's a relief," I said.

We ended up trying on practically every cap in the store; it took almost half an hour. The weird thing was that the Sweet brothers seemed more interested in finding me a cool baseball cap than trying some on for themselves. Finally we made our way over to the food court, where we just sat there at a round table *not* eating anything despite the delicious smells. At some point two things dawned on me: (1) I was no longer afraid that this was a painfully long setup that was going to suddenly end badly for me, and (2) trying on caps forever and then sitting silently at a table at the food court wasn't fun in the slightest. All the Sweet brothers did was sit there staring down kids from other towns and talking about some of the caps they'd just tried on, and after a while I couldn't even pretend to be interested and just sat there with my head in my hands. But there was one interesting thing that happened—classmates who were at the mall that afternoon not only seemed terrified of the Sweet brothers, but also were shocked that I was with them! It made me feel cool to be with them. Trent and his basketball buddies looked over at me with something like . . . respect?

"Do you have detention on Monday?" Hank asked me as we walked back to the bike rack. It was dark out at this point. A traffic helicopter flew overhead, toward the highway, and I realized that I hadn't even considered the fact that my parents might be worried about me.

"I'm going to make a huge maze tonight," Hugh said. "I guarantee you won't be able to solve it!"

"Does anyone else ever get detention?" I asked him.

"It's usually just me and Hank."

"You're a lifer like us!" Hank said, and we all high-fived.

Then Hugh absentmindedly started giving me a wedgie,

and I groaned on the inside, but Hank stopped him. "Not anymore," he told his brother really seriously. "We don't give wedgies to fellow lifers, right?"

"No, you're totally right," Hugh said, blushing. He smiled shyly at me. "Sorry, bud, it's like the reflex when the doc hits you on the knee with the rubber mallet, remember? Won't happen again, I promise."

"This is a really nice moment," I admitted, and we all kinda smiled at each other.

Even though the ride back was just as terrifying as the ride to the mall, something clicked in my brain as we pedaled back to the school, and I realized I was laughing out loud. The happy scene didn't last very long, however, because a couple of seconds later I swallowed a bug.

nineteen

THEY DROPPED ME OFF BACK at school and I ran home. It was almost dinnertime, but I had to stop at Drew's to tell him about my afternoon. I found him sitting up in Corbett Canyon, counting the mica stash. He looked kinda angry, actually.

"Forget the mica, and don't worry about the inventions contest, because everything just changed, big-time!" I shouted. "Guess what? I just hung out at the mall with the Sweet brothers—we're now friends!"

Drew's eyes widened.

"What? How?"

"They think I'm cool because I have detention."

"Aren't you scared of being around them?"

"You don't get it, that means we're in the clear with

170

them. If they like me, they have no choice but to like you!"

"That *is* great news!" Drew said, nodding his head.

"You just have to get detention next week," I added, and Drew's smile faded. "You know, so we can all hang out after school together."

"I'm not going to get detention on purpose, are you crazy?" he asked. "You shouldn't intentionally get detention like that. It's not good to get in trouble."

"Sometimes you have to do things you're not happy about in order to get what you want," I explained to him, feeling annoyed that he didn't understand how huge this all was.

"But the Sweet brothers are mean. You don't like them, do you?"

"You just haven't seen the Sweet brothers' good side. Just get detention this one time, and you'll see what I mean."

"I don't want detention," Drew said.

I groaned.

"Do you want to stay a nobody forever, Drew? What the heck have we been doing this whole time?"

"I don't want to be considered cool if it means giving myself detention and hanging out with the Sweet brothers."

"Look, Drew, we've worked so hard at thinking outside the box to solve our problems, and now we're so close to actually succeeding, can't you see that? What's wrong with you, man?"

"What's wrong is I'm starting to think there was never a box in the first place."

"Don't say that about the box!" I shouted. "What are you saying?"

"I'm saying I've helped you with all your ideas this whole time, and nothing's worked. Don't you get it, Peter? There is no box."

"Again, you're not quite getting the box thing, it's that—wait a sec, are you actually blaming our loserdom on me, Street Magic?"

He shrugged his shoulders.

"You've been the one calling all the shots," he said. "Your plans never work, and you just keep coming up with one lame plan after another. To be honest, I haven't even been on board with your last few schemes. Buying cigarettes? Befriending the Sweet brothers? Are you crazy?"

I could feel my face turning red.

"First of all, you're not even an inventor, so I don't get why you suddenly think you're the expert on inventing things, and second, I'm the one who's been coming up with schemes and you keep messing everything up," I explained—my voice was even a little shaky.

"How many failed schemes does it take for you to realize it's not working?"

"It took Thomas Edison a thousand tries before he got

the lightbulb right," I said.

"So you're saying you need a thousand tries?" Drew scoffed. "That would take forever, and we'd be dead by then."

"We'd only be dead because you'd just keep screwing up your role in these schemes!"

"Well, if you're so convinced that I'm the reason we're losers, and if I'm positive you're the reason, then maybe we should have an experiment and see what happens when we're not together," Drew suggested.

I gasped.

"Are you breaking up with me?" I asked him.

"No," Street Magic said quickly, but he was staring at the ground. "Consider this more like a time-out."

"Holy moly, you *are* breaking up with me!" I couldn't believe Drew. After everything I'd done for us. "Fine. Whatever you want, but I don't think you're going to like the result."

"I don't think *you're* going to like the result," he replied.

"Are you just going to repeat everything I say?"

"I don't know, am I going to repeat everything you say?" he replied.

I sighed. I hate when kids start repeating everything you say—there's no defense for it, really. "So what now?" I asked.

"We give it a few weeks," he replied. "By then, one of us should be popular, and then the other admits that he was wrong and we go back to being popular together."

"Deal," I said, and we shook on it. "But trust me, you're in over your head, pal. Honestly, I feel bad for you, Street Magic."

"And I you, Street Magic's Assistant," he replied.

We just stood there for a minute, not saying anything, before I finally looked down at my watch and realized it was now dinnertime. "I should probably go," I said.

"Bye, Peter!" Drew said cheerfully, before remembering that he was really mad at me.

And the experiment was officially under way.

It was chilly as I jogged home, and to take my mind off the cold, I replayed the conversation in my head. At first I got really mad at Drew again. How dare he suggest I was the reason for our problems! But then an uncomfortable feeling crept inside my bones, as I realized that this meant I was going to have to go it alone at school on Monday. And then I remembered that this was all Drew's fault, and I felt really angry at him again.

"How dare he!" I shouted out loud, and it made me blush, because whenever I see strangers shouting out loud to themselves on the street I think, man, what a weirdo.

I was positive my parents were going to be steaming out the ears that I was so late for dinner, but they didn't notice me when I entered the kitchen.

"Um, I'm home," I finally said. Still nothing. "Where's the funeral?"

"Your sister had her lucky pen stolen at school today," Mom said softly.

Sunny was pacing back and forth by the sink.

"I think whoever the thief is should be expelled when they catch him," Sunny said. "No question. I swear, if I find out who stole my pen—"

"Relax, it's just a pen," I said.

She glared at me.

"It's not just any old pen, it's the pen I've used to get straight A's for all of middle school. It's an official NASA astronaut's pen that I won, you can write upside down in space with it!"

"Well, that should narrow down the list of suspects—it has to be someone who owns a spaceship."

"You're an idiot."

"I was obviously kidding," I replied. "Which makes you a double idiot."

"Not if you consider that in math two negatives make a positive, in which case technically a double idiot's a good—"

"For the love of Pete, that's enough! Stop bickering, you two," Dad said, not peering up from his newspaper. "Just make sure you both keep a good eye on your things from now on."

"Why are you home so late?" Mom finally asked me.

"I did some work after detention," I said, blushing.

She smiled at me.

"See? Maybe detention's not a bad thing in the end."

"For once, I couldn't agree with you more," I said.

I went up to my bedroom after dinner and opened my closet to get my old winter jacket out. I figured since my fingertips still hadn't thawed from my jog home an hour earlier, it was now officially cold enough that I was going to have to start wearing it to school, even though I'd probably lose it in a week. I was shocked to find Drew's jacket on a coat hanger! I guess the thief hadn't stolen it, after all. I suddenly remembered that during the summer I'd accused Sunny a bunch of times of stealing my recorder. And then when I realized I'd been storing it up at Corbett Canyon, Dad shook his head at me and said that people who are suspicious all the time are suspicious because they lie all the time. And that those who rarely lie aren't often suspicious.

I didn't believe him.

twenty

I T FELT WEIRD TO WALK BY MYSELF to school the following Monday. Even though I was mad at Drew for
accusing me of being the source of all our troubles, I had
to admit that I already couldn't wait for the experiment to
be over so Drew and I could go back to being best friends.
What the heck was he thinking? He'd never been good
at coming up with ideas on his own. He was just going to
make a fool of himself, like that new kid last year, Pierre
something, who moved to Fenwick midway through fifth
grade. He tried to get everyone to like him the first day by
bringing in a box of fancy French cookies, and it worked
for a little while, but by the end of recess he'd run out
of cookies and everyone went back to not being friends
with him. He's not in middle school now, and nobody

knows what happened to him.

At the same time, I realized that I didn't have a solution, myself. I pictured the way classmates seemed shocked that I was with the Sweet brothers at the mall. None of them had tried to talk to Hugh and Hank, though. I thought about what Sunny had said about them—maybe she was right. In which case, being friends with the Sweet brothers would only solve the bullying problem, but me and Drew would still be losers. How could I use my new friendship with the Sweet brothers to become popular? I suddenly felt really depressed that there was no obvious answer, but it turned out the answer was right around the corner. I walked into the lobby before homeroom, and Trent immediately approached me.

"I saw you last week at the mall," he said.

"Oh yeah?" I scratched the top of my head. "I don't recall that at all."

"Were you with the Sweet brothers?"

"They're friends of mine," I said.

"Can you get me in tight with them?"

"I suppose I could try." At first I wanted to immediately bring him over to the Sweet brothers and introduce them, but then I thought, that would be the end of that, just like when poor ol' Pierre ran out of his fancy French cookies. "It's not that easy. I can't just introduce you right now—they might beat you up or something."

Trent looked scared.

"Don't worry," I added. "I'll figure something out. You just have to earn their respect like I did."

"How do I do that?"

"I think I have a plan," I said. "Are you free this afternoon?"

Trent nodded. The bell rang, and we trudged upstairs. I almost ran right into Sunny—she was lugging her yellow inventor's duffel bag around, even though she had her backpack on, too.

"Why are you carrying that thing around? That's what the cubbies are for."

"I was working on my prototype last night, genius," she said. "Besides, I'm not leaving my bag overnight here—there's a thief, remember?"

"The thief's not going to try to steal something from you again. It's like lightning—if you got struck once, then you probably won't get struck again."

"There's a forest ranger who got struck seven times, actually, it's in *Guinness Book of World Records*," she objected.

I rolled my eyes.

"Whatever—have fun lugging that thing around for the rest of your life."

* * *

When I showed up at social-studies class after lunch, Trent was sitting in his usual spot, staring intently at his desktop. I waited for Mrs. Farley to get into her lecture about whatever it was we were supposed to be learning before I commenced with what I later thought of as the conversation method. The teacher turned around to scribble something on the chalkboard, at which point I said loudly, "What's that, Trent?"

He looked up at me with a confused expression on his face.

"And so these people from this country attacked the people from this other country, and . . ." Mrs. Farley rambled on, writing some weird names I'd never heard of onto the chalkboard. Trent stared back down at his desktop.

"I'm sorry, come again, Trent?" I said.

Mrs. Farley turned around.

"No talking, boys," she said.

I shrugged my shoulders at the teacher and squinted at the chalkboard, scribbling lines into my notebook in a way that suggested from a distance that I was writing actual words. She went back to talking about some war or meeting overseas that took place a really long time ago, and I said a third time, "What did you just ask me, Trent?"

"I didn't say anything!" he said.

"I said, let's stop the chitchat, Trent," Mrs. Farley said.

"It's not me, teach!" Trent's face was turning bright red.

She sighed disappointedly at him, then resumed writing something on the chalkboard. I turned to Trent.

"What is it you're asking me?" I whispered loudly.

"It's not me, I'm not saying anything," Trent shouted. "What the heck's wrong with you?"

"That's it, you two," Mrs. Farley snapped. "You can continue your conversation in detention after school."

Will do, I thought.

"Mrs. Farley, Street Magic's Assistant here keeps talking to me, but I swear I'm not saying anything!"

"And how do you respond to that, Street Mag—er, Mr. Lee?" she asked me.

"Agree to disagree," I said, trying to look confused. "I was merely asking Trent to repeat what he was asking me."

She sighed, then turned and continued writing things on the chalkboard.

"What's wrong with you?" Trent whispered to me.

"Shh," I whispered back. "You're going to get us in more trouble."

Trent's face turned red.

When the bell rang at the end of the day, I practically sprinted off to detention class. As I turned the corner, I almost crashed into Sunny, who was sitting at a desk in the middle of the hallway, wearing her stupid hall-monitor sash.

"Are you still trying to glom on to me?" she said.

"No!"

"Well, you can't run in the halls," she said. "I'm going to have to write you up."

"But it's after school!" I shouted. "Why do they need a hall monitor after school, anyway?"

"I volunteered," she replied. "We have band rehearsal soon, so I figured I'd squeeze in some minutes."

"That is incredibly nerdy, you know that?"

"Why are you running in the first place?"

"I have detention," I said with a big smile on my face.

"And you're happy about that? Right, so *I'm* the nerd. . . ."

"I'm proud of you—it takes courage to be able to admit something so lame about yourself," I said, taking off.

"You know that's not what I meant—*slow down!*" she shouted after me, but I ignored her.

I opened the door to room 12, and Trent was already there, staring at his desk in the back row. He stared at desks a lot, for some reason. He looked up and waved me over— already the power of the detention force field was working!

"Aloha, Trent," I said. "So what was that thing you were asking me in class earlier?"

"Dude, I wasn't saying a word, you were talking to me!"

"I'm kidding. I did it on purpose."

"Why would you do that?" he asked, fuming.

"You said you wanted to get in tight with the Sweet brothers, didn't you?"

"What does that have to do with anything?" he asked, but then the door opened, and in walked Hugh and Hank.

"Hey, guys," I said cheerfully. "Do you know Trent?"

They glared at him.

"Did you come here to bring us our allowance?" Hugh asked him.

Trent looked at me. I shook my head, so Trent shook his head at them.

"What are you in here for?" Hank asked.

Trent looked at me again.

"Let's just say the teachers aren't crazy about him at this point," I said. "And leave it at that."

Hugh laughed, and sat down next to Trent, who noticeably stiffened. But by the end of detention it seemed they were getting along famously, and Trent leaned over and whispered to me, "Thanks, bro. So you think they like me?"

"Honestly, I don't think so," I said.

"How can you tell? We were talking the entire detention!"

"I know those two. They're not sure about you. Just keep getting detentions and I'll work on them from my end."

Trent sighed, and I patted him on the shoulder.

"It's a good start, I know they'll change their mind about you eventually. But for this to work, you can't tell anyone how I'm helping you. If the Sweet brothers were to find out, we'd both be toast, and I can't have that."

"I owe you one, man," he replied.

The detention theory worked! Maybe Drew was right, in a way. We had to break up in order for me to figure out how to finally solve things.

twenty-one

I GOT HOME FROM SCHOOL AND Mom was sitting in the living room with her sewing kit out. She waved me over. "Look, I'm making you something."

A pile of my clothes was lying in a heap next to her. I frowned.

"You're not trying to make me clothes again, are you?" I asked her.

When I was in fourth grade, I went through a mini growth spurt and my mom was upset that clothes cost so much, so she tried making me clothes that winter. I went to school in sweaters that looked okay in the morning, but if they got caught on a nail or on the edge of a desk, they would unravel, and I'd come home with half a sleeve missing and a ball of yarn trailing behind me like a colored tail. She would've kept making me shoddy clothes for the rest of my life, but then I stopped growing and haven't grown since, so I guess there's one good thing about being so little.

"I'm sewing your initials on every piece of clothing you own," she said. "I got an email today from the vice-principal. He said they were emailing all parents to alert them to this thief problem at your school."

"Why are you sewing my initials into my underwear?" I asked her, and she stared back at me. "How could I ever possibly have my underwear stolen in school?"

She frowned.

"I suppose that would be a little difficult," she admitted. "But better safe than sorry. Think about those poor students who have had iPods and cell phones stolen. Imagine losing a cell phone—those are expensive!"

"First I'd have to imagine actually owning a cell phone," I said.

"You know what I mean."

I sighed.

"I feel sorry for whoever it is that's stealing these things," she said.

"Are you crazy?" I asked her. "You feel sorry for someone who steals everyone's stuff?"

"The thief is clearly a very sad young person crying out

for help," she said. "Imagine what is driving someone to steal like that."

"I hear it more like someone crying out for a beating," I said.

She shook her head sadly at me and went back to sewing. I picked up a pile of my T-shirts and started walking away.

"What's going on?" Sunny asked, entering the living room.

"I'm stitching Peter's initials into his underwear," Mom explained.

Sunny got a big grin on her face.

"That's a good idea," she said, patting me on the back. It stung. "Then when he gets confused, he can just look at his underwear and remember his own name."

"That is really funny," I said, staring at her. "Don't you have to study for your SATs? They're only three years away."

"He's right, Sunny. If you have spare time right now, you could do a practice test. Hey, Peter, look," she said, holding up a pair of my underwear. "I sewed a little smiley face next to your initials! Isn't that adorable?"

"Great," I said, rolling my eyes. "I'm sure everyone in gym class will love it."

For once I actually knew that I had an English test the next day, so I took the digital camera into my dad's office that night and uploaded all the pics I'd taken in my classes the last few weeks. I made separate folders for each class, then opened up a slideshow of the English chalkboard photos. Uh-oh. They were low resolution, and when I zoomed in, the writing on the chalkboard got all grainy. I tried to copy what I could make out into my notebook, which felt annoying—I was ending up having to take notes, anyway.

For the rest of study time, I worked on my plan to start using the detention theory at school, brainstorming ways to get popular kids into detention. I'd already developed the conversation method, but the problem with it was that it gave me a detention, too, and as useful as detention was these days, I didn't want it to last forever. I thought about it for a while and eventually came up with what I called the passing-notes method. The goal was to make it look like my targets were passing notes in class, which is something the teachers at Fenwick Middle hate more than anything, it seems.

That night I sat at my desk during study time, figuring out who I should frame next. I made a chart of who I figured were the most important popular people in the sixth grade, listing the reasons why being friends with them could help me. Here's an example of what the finished chart looked like:

<u>Target</u>: Donnie Christopher

<u>Reason</u>: Friends with Carson and the brainiac crew. Has a gigantic head. I already have T.A.G. class with Carson, but since I'm not popular, he can't see how smart I am. The key is to get Donnie on my side, too, then Carson and the other genius robots will like me.

<u>Target</u>: Sally Leathers

<u>Reason</u>: Friends with Angie, who has the parties that all the popular people go to. Get in tight with Sally, and Angie will have to invite me.

Those were the main targets besides Trent, who I'd already worked my magic with. I also planned on framing Heidi Markowitz because she was friends with the field-hockey girls, and Shawn Jacobs, who hung out with all the skateboarders, and Dylan Armstrong, a Hemenway kid who actually wasn't all that popular, but I'd heard that he owned a snake that ate live mice, and I'd always wanted to see that in person.

The next morning I raced around the hall before first period looking for the Sweet brothers. How things had changed—now I was actually *trying* to find them instead of avoiding them at all costs. I saw Hank shoving Donnie, into his locker, and I ran right up to them.

"Hey, Hank," I said, and we high-fived. "See you this afternoon."

Sure enough, Donnie approached me just before English class.

"Hey, Peter—you're friends with the Sweet brothers?"

"Sure, we go way back."

"Can you get them off my back?"

"I'll see what I can do."

I sat in class trying to come up with a simple fake note. I worried that I'd never bothered to check out Donnie's handwriting style, so I ended up writing in a robot font:

This adult human bores me. I am wasting my internal lithium batteries listening to this unintelligent human instructor tell me things I already know. I will keep my eyes open but otherwise put myself in sleep mode. —Donnie

I carefully folded it into a self-contained square, the way I'd seen girls do when they expertly pass notes all class long. The plan was to drop off the note somewhere in plain sight so Mr. Vensel would find it once class was over. When the bell rang, I stayed in my seat while everyone else got up. As the students filed toward the exit, I made the drop-off as subtly as possible, but it wasn't even necessary. Mr. Vensel had his back to me, erasing stuff he'd written on the chalkboard. Was it really this easy? I wondered.

The Sweet brothers and Trent were waving me over from the back of the detention room when I arrived at the end of the day, but I told them I had to figure out some homework first and sat down by myself at the front. The sound of the buses pulling out of the lot filled me with sadness—my plan hadn't worked. But then a moment later the door opened, and in walked a terrified Donnie, who immediately gaped at the sight of the massive Sweet brothers in the back. I nodded at the empty seat next to me, which he took gratefully.

"What's the human Pez dispenser doing here?" Hank snarled at Donnie.

I patted the human Pez dispenser on the back.

"Let's just say this guy and Mr. Vensel are no longer on speaking terms," I said, and Hank seemed impressed.

Donnie looked confused. I leaned over and whispered, "The key to getting them off your back is to get to know them better."

"Thanks," he whispered, and I hid the smile forming on the inside of my mouth.

By framing students into detention, I quickly became an expert on what would get you in trouble and exactly how much trouble it would get you in. I even made a little guide on a piece of paper that I kept hidden in my desk drawer at home, which looked like this:

The Conversation Method = 1 detention
The Passing-Notes Method = 3 detentions
The Having-Candy-in-Class Method = 3 detentions
The Tic-Tac-Toe Method = 1 detention
The Writing-on-the Desk Method = 2 detentions

I preferred leaving fake notes, because it was easy and I could prepare the fake note the night before. The candy method was equally effective, but I didn't use it much (because I hate wasting perfectly good candy, obviously). The tic-tac-toe method was easier to prepare than coming up with a fake note—I'd just draw a bunch of games of tic-tac-toe on a piece of paper and then at the bottom write something like "Shawn Rules!" but it was worth only one detention. That it was even worth detention says something about how much teachers hate tic-tac-toe—they hate that kids don't pay attention, but they hate it even more if you don't pay attention because you're playing a game that's so stupid it always ends in a tie. Writing on the desk was risky—basically I'd just write someone's initials followed by a really positive word and an exclamation point (like "H.M. Rules!") on my desk. When the teacher saw it, they'd assume Heidi Markowitz had sat there, and she would get two detentions just like that. But it was risky—it depended on the teacher not paying close enough attention to realize I'd sat there.

What I eventually figured out was that I could combine methods to get students in even more trouble. For example, if I wanted to get Heidi Markowitz into detention for a week, all I had to do was use the passing-notes method, but have the note read, "Kerri, I am loving eating candy right now, do you want to play tic-tac-toe? —Heidi." And like that, boom, Heidi had seven detentions!

I realized that I didn't even have to use my friendship with the Sweets to get closer to popular people. Just being in detention with them made us suddenly chummy with each other. It was like there was an invisible force field surrounding room 12 that made everyone inside it get along, no matter what. I used the passing-notes method to frame Sally into detention, and when she showed up I just sat next to her and we chatted as if we were back in elementary school together. By the end of detention I even impressed Sally when she discovered how talented I was at drawing her favorite animal in the entire world—the unicorn.

I made sure to draw Sally a unicorn every detention—I figured the key to getting invited to Angie's parties was my expertise at drawing unicorns, and I tried to work in subtle hints as she sat there watching me produce art.

"You're so good at drawing them," she said one time. "Don't forget the tail this time."

"Of course," I said, scribbling in a silky tail. "You know, Sally, in addition to drawing, I'm also really good at interior decorating—you know, for, like, awards ceremonies and, um, more casual social gatherings."

"What are you talking about?" she asked.

Okay, so my hints weren't working, but the fact that we were friendly made me think it was just a matter of time before I got invited to a party.

No matter what type of students they were—nerds, jocks, bullies, or princesses—they all were instantly friendly with me in detention. Trent started saying hi to me every morning in the lobby before homeroom, Heidi waved as I passed her locker between periods, and even Donnie and his brainiac Hemenway pals nodded at me in the hallways. My plan was *working*!

Meanwhile, from what I could gather watching him in the hallways and during lunch, Drew's only plan for becoming popular was going up to popular kids between classes with a hand covering an eye and asking them if they'd come across his left contact lens. I guess there was one perk to being a nobody—no one but me seemed to know that he had perfect vision. I snuck up on him after third period one morning.

"You do realize that it's pretty ridiculous to ask some-one if they happened to see a contact lens on the floor," I pointed out to him. "How would anyone ever stumble across a tiny piece of see-through plastic on the ground?"

"Well, that's what makes my strategy so sound," Drew said after a couple of seconds. "I don't actually want them to find a contact lens, now, do I?"

He had a point there.

"Are you just going to ask kids to help you find your con-tacts for the rest of your life?" I asked him.

"At some point they're going to add up how much time we've spent looking for my contacts over the years and real-ize we've kinda become close friends," he replied.

"That has to be the lamest idea I've ever heard in my life."

"You sit by yourself at lunch, so I don't think you're in a position to mock me," he replied.

"You sit by yourself, too!" I said, but then at lunch I sat down at our old table and watched in horror as Drew pulled the ol' lost contact method on Trent's table, and they had no choice but to let him sort of sit with them. I say "sort of" because he didn't eat anything, and technically he didn't ever sit in a chair—for the entire lunch period he was on his knees, crawling around their table in circles, pretending to look for his left contact lens. At first I felt kinda bad for him, he looked so pitiful, but then Trent got out of his chair and started looking, too. I sighed.

I turned back to my tray and made eye contact with one of Heidi's Hemenway girlfriends, who looked at me, then at the empty chairs around me, and even though it made no sense I suddenly picked up my banana and pretended talking into it as if it was a cell phone, laughing into the peel at something an imaginary friend had said.

Okay, so trying to get popular people to like you by having them help you find your lost contact lens was the *second* stupidest method in the world.

twenty-two

IT TURNED OUT I WAS CELEBRATING my victory over Drew a little too early, because on Monday morning I overheard everyone talking about another party at Angie's on Saturday that I hadn't been invited to! Trent had gone, of course. So had Donnie. Even the Sweet brothers had gone! Which meant that I wasn't becoming popular through the detention theory like I'd thought. Heck, I was no different from poor ol' Pierre Something and his box of fancy French cookies, and like Pierre Something, I'd run out of cookies. It simply wasn't enough to just get them all in detention. I needed to step it up with Sally in order for Angie to consider inviting me to her next party, then everyone would mistakenly assume I was popular like them and all would be right in the world. I made a mental note as I walked to detention that I was going to draw Sally the most amazing unicorn ever; she'd be so impressed and grateful for my art skills that, heck, she'd invite me to the next party herself.

I tried to picture what the most amazing unicorn ever would look like, but at first my ideas were kinda pitiful. A two-horned unicorn? Nope. A three-horned unicorn? I pictured it and it looked like a really skinny triceratops. I reminded myself to think outside the box, and that's when the solution came to me—the answer wasn't adding details to a regular unicorn, but to use multiplication. I'd simply draw her a picture of a tiny teenaged unicorn riding atop another unicorn. That's right . . . *double unicorn!* I guess there is a time and place for math in the real world, after all, I thought. I showed up at room 12 that afternoon and immediately saw that my fears were true. Hank was talking to Trent, and even worse—Donnie was already drawing a unicorn for Sally!

It suddenly occurred to me that maybe drawing unicorns wasn't the key to getting invited to parties on the weekends.

I sat down at a desk and nobody even looked up at me because I was no longer their savior; I was just another kid in detention, that's all.

A minute later Hugh walked in, and he looked really mad. I felt nervous for some reason. "What's going on?" Trent asked him.

"The thief stole my baseball cap," he replied.

"I thought you lost your hat a long time ago?" I asked him.

"That was Hank's hat," Hugh said. "How could you confuse us?"

"Well, you are twins—," I started saying, but he glared at me.

"We have to catch the thief," Hank said, pounding a fist against a desk. Mr. Tinsley looked up at him. "Sorry, teach."

"It's impossible," Trent said. "There are three hundred students in the school, how could we possibly figure out who the thief is?"

Hugh groaned, but my heart skipped a beat. Maybe this was an opening, a way I could get everyone to really like me? My unicorn-drawing plan was a bust, and Trent and Donnie were just as chummy with the Sweet brothers as I was, so, without thinking, I said, "It'd be pretty easy to deduce who did it, actually."

"I'm listening," Hugh said, staring at me.

Mr. Tinsley got up from his seat. "I have a student conference, but I'll be right next door—if I hear anything, you all get another detention. Everyone stay in your seats, and I'll be back before the end of the period."

With the teacher gone, I went up to the front of the class and got their attention by scraping my nails down the chalkboard. They winced.

"That wasn't really necessary," Hank said. "We were already paying attention to you."

"Anyway—look," I said. "The first thing we have to do is narrow down the list of possible suspects."

"But the thief could be anyone," Hugh said.

"Are you the thief?" I asked him.

"Why would I steal my own hat?"

"How about you, Sally—are you the thief?"

"I didn't steal my own key chain!"

"So that's two of the three hundred we just ruled out," I said.

They all murmured approvingly, recognizing my genius deducting skills.

"See, you're looking at it the wrong way. To narrow down the list of possible suspects, we need to make lists." I took out my notebook and opened to the first blank page— which, sadly, given the fact that it was over a month into the school year, was page 3—and started ripping out pages and passing them around. Once everyone had a page, I said, "Okay, for a couple of minutes, work on a list of possible enemies. Then we'll go over the lists and see if any of the names turn up more than once, and those would then be our main suspects."

"That's a good idea," Donnie admitted.

I started feverishly writing down names of people who'd picked on me, or laughed at me, or ignored me the start of school, which was practically everyone. I looked up and noticed nobody else was writing. Instead they were all staring at each other with confused looks on their faces.

"Why aren't you writing any names down?" I asked.

"I don't have any enemies," Sally said, and I felt my ears redden.

"Sally's the most popular girl in the entire school, practically," Hank said. "Her birthday party at Angie's house this weekend was the biggest party, ever."

"Same goes for Trent," Donnie added. "The basketball guys rule the school."

"And everyone respects you, Donnie," Trent said. "You're like the Hemenway version of the Human Calculator."

Frankly, I was disgusted that they were saying this. Were they really this full of themselves? I looked over at the Sweet brothers and was appalled to see that they were drawing mazes instead of making a list!

"Really, you two don't have any enemies?" I asked. "You guys bully everyone in school!"

"Exactly," Hugh said. "But we're equal-opportunity bullies, we bully everyone, so we'd have to list everyone, which would be a complete waste of time."

"Well, you have a point there," I admitted. I turned to

Sally. "Did everyone in school go to your party, Sally?"

I blushed, realizing I was pointing out that the thief would probably be someone who didn't go to the party, and I'd momentarily forgotten that I was one of those people!

"Of course not. Angie's basement can't hold that many people. You know that."

How would I know that, I wondered?

"Street Magic's Assistant has a point—wouldn't people who didn't get invited to your party have a reason to resent you?" Donnie asked, and I started feeling nervous again.

"They probably didn't even know about it," Sally replied.

"Yeah, they're probably doing other stuff and could care less about going anyway," Trent said.

"This is too hard," Sally said. "I can't handle thinking about such big numbers. I can't remember everyone who didn't go to my party. You're good at thinking about this stuff, Peter, just try to remember who didn't go."

I blushed. What the heck was she talking about? Didn't she know I didn't go to it, or any party Angie and Sally ever had? Or was this a trap? I tried to keep a straight face.

"You want me to remember who wasn't at your last party?" I asked.

"Yeah, I was busy hosting the thing, you'd know better than I would."

It was weird—I felt lucky and relieved that they

mistakenly thought I went to these parties, but at the same time it almost made me feel more mad that they didn't even realize I hadn't gone.

"Well, you can't accuse us, Peter, because we hung out at the party, remember?" Hugh said. "Didn't we?"

I panicked that he was going to realize I wasn't there. I had to mention a detail about the party to prove I was there, but I had no idea what a middle-school party looked like, having never been to one; all I had to go on was me and Drew's fake party. I pictured Drew in a dress, sitting up in Corbett Canyon, and sighed. I took a stab in the dark. "Oh yeah, we were drinking that weird drink together."

He didn't say anything at first, and I was positive he was going to point out that the rule at Angie's house was that they served only solids, no liquids, and I'd be busted.

"Right!" Hugh said, a moment later.

I exhaled softly.

"That drink was gross, it's safe to admit now, right Sally?" Trent said.

"Oh, be quiet," Sally said, smiling.

"I was too hyper from that weird drink so I probably didn't notice everyone. Instead, let's try another method," I said, ripping out a new page and crumbling up the previous list.

"No more lists, this feels like work," Sally whined, and

she got her wish, because a moment later the bell rang.

"To be continued," I said, but everyone was rushing out the door already.

I suddenly got an idea, so instead of heading home I jogged through the school to the top of the back stairway, where I saw Sunny lugging her yellow duffel bag out of the library.

"What happened—did you fall asleep?" I asked her. "School's been out for over an hour."

"I was doing extra work on my invention, jailbird," she said. "How was detention? I'm surprised you've survived this long."

"Actually, I get along great with the Sweet brothers," I said proudly.

"That's a good thing, because you'll already have friends if you ever end up going to prison."

"I was thinking the exact same—," I started saying, before realizing she was being sarcastic. I headed into the library and found Ms. Schoonmaker pushing all the chairs into the table. She looked up at me. "I just had an idea. If I could catch the thief of Fenwick Middle, could I get out of detention on Wednesdays so I can come back to T.A.G. sooner?"

She sighed.

"That's not how it works, unfortunately," she said. "Have

you ever heard the word 'ownership'? That's what you're doing by going to detention—you're taking responsibility for your actions."

"Have you ever heard of the word 'parole'?" I replied. "Or the phrase, 'Time off for good behavior'?"

"You're not in prison," she said. "I'm sorry, Peter, there's nothing I can do about your detention situation."

I started heading back out.

"Peter," she said, and I stopped. "You can still participate in the inventors' fair if you can work on a prototype in your spare time. That's the best I can do."

On the way home I couldn't help myself and stopped by Drew's house. I figured even though we'd agreed to separate, maybe he'd beg me to take him back. Maybe he'd be up for joining the club in detention and things would be perfect. He was sitting in the middle of the backyard, counting clovers.

"How many did you collect?" I asked.

"Not many."

"But there are tons of clovers all around you. It would take forever."

"I'm not exactly in a rush," he said, not looking at me.

I waited ten seconds for him to break down in tears and beg me to take him back, but he just kept staring at the grass.

"Speaking of collecting, I kinda feel like counting the mica," I said.

He looked at me with a puzzled expression on his face.

"Why? You hate the mica."

"I don't know, I just feel like it," I said, and started climbing up the ladder to Corbett Canyon. At the top of the ladder I looked down at Drew—he was staring at his clovers. This made me a little mad, I was only pretending to be interested in the mica to make him happy, and he didn't even care. I went inside and opened up the safe—and gasped.

The bag was gone!

"Where's the mica?" I shouted. He raced up the ladder.

"It should be right there," he said.

I sat down in the middle of the tree house.

"The thief stole our mica collection," I said.

"That's impossible, there's a lock on the safe," Drew replied.

"I can't believe this happened," I said, and kicked at the wall.

"You don't care," Drew said. "You're the one who wanted to chuck the mica."

"I do care!" I shouted. "Now I'm going to really have to catch the thief. If you joined my detention club, you could help us solve the mystery of the thief."

"Oh, so you're in a club now?" he said, and climbed back down the ladder without looking at me.

"And to think I even felt sorry for you," I called out after him, but he was gone.

A minute later he climbed back into the tree house and sat next to me.

"I thought you were going somewhere," I said.

"Well, I live here," he said.

"Oh—right."

We didn't say anything. It started feeling really awkward sitting in the tiny tree house together and not talking like that, so eventually I left.

twenty-three

I WAS WORRIED THAT EVERYONE IN detention had forgotten that I was kind of leading the thief investigation, but when I showed up the next afternoon they were all waiting for me. "So what do we do now?" Hugh asked.

"Today we're going to profile the thief," I said.

"You mean, like on TV?" Trent asked.

"Exactly. All those shows are about first figuring out what kind of person the criminal is—that's what we have to do. So here's a question: Who would want to steal stuff from us?"

"Here's what a thief would be like," Sally said, counting off her fingers on one hand. "He's probably a loner. He doesn't hang out with anyone on weekends or after school. He does bad in classes. He's not athletic. Nobody likes him."

I reddened—basically she was describing me to a T.

"How do we even know it's a guy?" Trent asked.

"A girl would never steal your basketball," Sally scoffed.

"Why would a guy want to steal a stupid horseshoe key chain?"

"It's not stupid!"

"Stop fighting," I said. "It could be a boy or girl. And yeah, that's the obvious choice, that it's a loner, but it could just as easily be someone popular. Maybe it's a popular person jealous of an even more popular person."

Donnie was holding his temples, as if his gigantic brain was about to melt from information overload. "So you're saying it could be a loner, but it could also be a popular person. It could be a boy, but it could also be a girl. It could be an athlete, or it could be a worm. That's not narrowing the profile down at all. We're not getting anywhere!"

"You're being impatient, we've only just started profiling the thief. Remember, it usually takes an entire TV episode to do this," I said.

"Forget the profiling thing," Hugh said, slamming his fist on the desk. "Donnie's right, what we need is action."

"Now that's what I'm talking about," Trent said, punching Hugh in the shoulder.

Mr. Tinsley shook his head at Trent, but didn't take off

his headphones. A second later he went back to grading papers. I turned to Hugh.

"We just have to keep coming up with a profile of the thief and—"

"Give it a rest, Peter. We need to do this the American way, with action. What does the U.S. do when we have a problem? We kick butt and take names later!" Hugh said, and everyone nodded.

"U.S.A.," Hank started chanting, and everyone joined him, and within seconds it sounded like we were at the Olympics.

"U.S.A.! U.S.A.! U.S.A.! U.S.A.! U.S—"

"Knock it off!" Mr. Tinsley hollered.

"Tomorrow," Hugh whispered to us, "we start taking the fight to the thief."

This didn't sound good.

Taking the fight to the thief basically meant shaking down anyone that made the mistake of crossing paths with the Sweet brothers between classes. Hugh and Hank started conducting random locker searches on Wednesday by sneaking up on kids at their lockers and between periods forced random students to empty their pockets.

"Why'd you pat him down?" I asked, after Hank let a sixth grader run off.

"He looked away from me when I made eye contact with him," he said.

"Everyone looks away from you when you make eye contact with them," I pointed out. He shrugged. "Plus, you're twice his size."

"The thief didn't steal my sweatshirt, he stole my hat— look closely at him—see? Our heads are similarly sized," Hank said. "He probably wears my hat in bed every night. I can just see it. Let's go grab him again."

"You're getting out of control," I said, but he wouldn't listen.

I had to admit, though, patting down random kids seemed to make everyone feel better about things. It wasn't getting us closer to finding the thief, but at least we were doing something hands-on about it. At the end of the day Trent came up behind me.

"Donnie said he has a really good idea for how to catch the thief," he said.

My stomach fell. Being in charge of the thief investigation was my job!

"Hurry up," Hugh shouted when me and Trent got to detention. Everyone else was there already, huddled around Donnie's desk.

"So what's your great idea?" I asked him, unable to hide my jealousy, but luckily nobody noticed. Donnie took out his copy of last year's Hemenway Elementary face book and a copy of last year's Fenwick Elementary face book (which he'd borrowed from Carson) from his schoolbag and laid them out on his desk. He motioned to Hugh, who pulled out his copy of last year's Fenwick Middle yearbook and handed it to me.

"What is this?" I asked.

"No more random searches," he said, and everyone nodded.

"I was saying that the other day," I kinda shouted.

"Quiet, Peter, we're finally making headway here," Sally said, shushing me.

My ears boiled.

"We're going to use traditional means of deduction," Donnie said. "I got this idea because I'm on the yearbook committee. We have before us the name and photo of every student who goes to the school right now. We're going to one by one look at each photo and discuss the possibility of whether they're the thief or not until we narrow the list of suspects down to one person."

"But that's what I was trying to do with the profiling," I said.

"No, your idea was to try to get inside the mind of a thief or whatever," Sally said. "And all we got out of that was that the thief might be a girl, but it might also be a boy, or a jock, or an unathletic person, or someone in band—"

"Okay, let's start with the sixth grade, so let's look at the fifth graders last year," Trent said. "Then we'll look at the seventh and eighth graders."

They edged me out and started whispering about the different students. I couldn't believe it—they were treating Donnie like the leader all of a sudden! I picked up Hugh's middle-school yearbook. I'd never seen one before. I started flipping through it. Maybe Donnie was right. I suddenly had this feeling that if I stared into the eyes of the thief, even in a school picture, I'd be able to tell. I was good at reading Drew by just staring at his eyeballs, so maybe I had an undiscovered talent for it. For the first time I saw that Sunny really was the president of all the clubs—every group photo had her in front holding the sign saying the name of the club. I sighed and turned to the first page of student photos. The very first person, Anna Ardsley, was smiling at me. She looked sketchy because her eyes were black (although I couldn't say for sure, given that the picture was in black and white), and I felt a chill in my chest. Was I staring at the thief?

"Guys!" I whispered. "I think I found the—"

But then I looked at the next student photo, Craig Bailey, and he definitely looked like he could be the thief, too, even more so than Anna. I looked into the eyes of a few more students. They all looked kinda guilty, if you asked me.

I exhaled.

The others weren't faring much better. They'd get excited about a potential suspect but then realize they were listing the same reasons they'd come up with about the previous student, and in the end they'd mark in red pen next to the photo, "Maybe."

"Any good suspects yet?" I asked.

"Maybe we're missing something staring right at us," Trent admitted, scratching his head. "They're all pretty good."

"This kid seems the creepiest, though," Donnie said, pointing at a picture of Pierre Something. Poor kid couldn't catch a break, even after he was long gone.

I snickered at Donnie.

"He doesn't even go to school here," I said. "Nice investigative skills."

"I wish he still went here," Sally said sadly. "Remember when he brought in those really fancy cookies?"

"Once—and then nobody talked to him again!" I noted.

"That doesn't mean the cookies weren't amazing," she said.

I sighed and turned back to the middle-school yearbook and flipped through the pages. Pictures of teachers wearing wigs on Halloween for the annual costume pageant, some sports photos, more class pictures, a two-page spread of the school itself, and then I came across a strange page with no pictures on it.

Across the top it read, "Last Will and Testament."

"Hey, Hugh, what's this?" I asked, sliding the book his way.

"That's this stupid thing where departing eighth graders leave behind their most prized possessions to someone in the sixth or seventh grade. They don't actually leave it behind, it's just an excuse to throw a shout out to someone in the yearbook," he said, before turning back to the Fenwick Elementary face book again. I read some of the entries in the Last Will and Testament.

I, Jared Kinesky, leave behind my Nalgene water bottle to Toby Moller, who was always so thirsty.

I, Ava Bernstein, leave behind my lunch box for Suzy Comer, who also thinks it's funny.

"Stop wasting your time, Peter," Trent barked. "We should all be focusing on discussing these mug shots."

"What's the point? You even just said that everyone looks kinda guilty," I snapped. "I'm telling you, the key is to work on the profile of the thief."

"We've already done that, and it was useless," Hank said.

"But he's right," Sally said. "This isn't working!"

"Fine, Peter, tell us again what the profile of the thief should be," Donnie said, clearly angry that I was competing with him for control of the investigation.

"Okay, we know that the thief is someone who's stealing stuff from everyone, so he has a big collection of stuff that he's hiding somewhere, for one thing," I said. "And the thief is definitely skilled at the art of hiding and deception, two. And—"

"Oh my God," Donnie said, slapping his forehead.

"What?" Sally asked.

Everyone looked at Donnie. He looked like he'd seen a ghost. More specifically, he looked like he'd seen a ghost standing behind me, and it made me shiver.

"Don't you get it?" he asked everyone.

I suddenly felt afraid. Very afraid.

"Get what?" Trent asked.

"I wish people would be more direct in here," Hank whined.

Donnie rolled his eyes.

"Peter's the thief!" he said.

I was relieved—for a second I thought he'd figured out that I was framing everybody into detention. I laughed out loud.

216

"Why would I describe myself if I was the thief?" I said.

"No, it makes perfect sense," Hugh said. "Peter's a magician, which means he knows how to make things disappear."

"I'm just an assistant," I said softly.

"On top of that, he was the best collector back in elementary school," Trent noted.

"He still collects!" Sally shouted.

"And what are thieves, but illegal collectors?" Hank said, nodding.

"I'm not sure that's Webster's definition of—," I started, but Sally cut me off.

"Oh my God—of course, Peter even got caught already. Angie told me he got detention for stealing chemicals from science class."

"Angie talked about me?" I asked, but everyone was staring at me. "Look, I was borrowing them. What? There's a big difference. Why can't anyone understand that?"

The Sweet brothers stared at me. I held my hands out.

"I swear to you, I'm not the thief," I said. The weird thing was that even though I really wasn't the thief, I felt kinda like I was lying as I said it.

"But you fit the profile," Donnie said. "You're the only student at Fenwick Middle who fits the profile perfectly."

"What can I do to prove I'm not the thief?" I asked.

"The only thing you *can* do is find the thief," Hugh said.

"That's what I've been trying to this whole time."

"You're not going to be able to, because you're the thief!" Trent shouted.

"Let's call the principal," Sally said. "Where the heck is Mr. Tinsley?"

"I swear I'm not the thief," I repeated.

"Here's the deal," Hugh said, stamping his fist on the desk. "You have till Monday to find the thief and get our stuff back, especially my hat, and if you can't, we're going to turn you in to the principal."

"I'm telling you, I'm not—"

But by then they'd stopped listening to me. Mr. Tinsley finally walked in at that point, apologizing for being late, and I could feel everyone's eyes on me as if a half dozen magnifying glasses were being aimed at my back. Sally poked me in the ribs a minute later. I turned around.

"Could you draw me a unicorn?" she asked.

"Are you crazy?" I whispered. "You just accused me of being the thief."

"It's apples and oranges. You being the thief doesn't make you any less qualified to draw me a unicorn, does it?"

I sighed and started drawing her a stupid unicorn.

It was windy as I walked home after detention. I couldn't believe that things had somehow gotten worse. This was all the thief's fault. Now I really did need to catch him, but it seemed impossible. I kicked a rock down the street and replayed what had happened in detention; I had to admit, it kinda made sense that they'd think I could be the thief. I *was* the best collector in school, I *was* the best possible suspect, really. Nobody else was a magician, and a collector, and—I froze in my tracks, suddenly realizing who the real thief was.

It was Drew!

twenty-four

B Y THE TIME I GOT TO DREW'S HOUSE, it was dark out, but I didn't care. I stomped through the backyard and, sure enough, the Coleman lantern was on up in the tree house, and I could see Drew sitting inside, probably hatching a plan to steal back his winter jacket from me.

"Get down here!" I shouted.

Drew peeked out the window at me, then climbed down from Corbett Canyon. I went over and started shaking him by his shoulders.

"Are you insane? Why would you steal from people?" I shouted. "Do you have any idea how much trouble you're in right now?"

"What are you talking about? Get off me!"

"Everyone in detention thinks I'm the thief, but the truth

is you're the thief—admit it!"

"I'm not the thief, Peter!" he cried.

"Who else would steal our mica collection? You wanted it for yourself this whole time. And you're mad that I made friends through detention and was winning the experiment, and sure enough, everyone in detention has gotten stuff stolen! You said so yourself how much you hated the Sweet brothers!"

"First of all, yes, I have the mica," he said. "But I hid it from you so you wouldn't throw it out! Why would I steal it? It's in my tree house."

"Oh," I said. "But okay, so what were you doing up there just now? It's cold, you were plotting to steal your jacket back from me, weren't you? Fess up!"

"I wasn't, and besides—it's my jacket, Peter."

"I knew it—you're never going to let that go!" I said. "I can't believe I didn't figure this out sooner. You fit the profile perfectly. You're a collector, and a magician, and—"

"Well then, *you* fit the profile, too."

We stared at each other. Like I'd said before, best friends can read each other's eyes, and I realized he was telling the truth. I felt relieved and, I hate to admit it, kinda disappointed at the same time even though it meant my best friend wasn't the thief.

I sighed.

"I'm sorry," I said.

"You've changed, Peter. You're hanging out with the Sweet brothers, you get detention on purpose, and now you accuse me of being the thief? I don't know you anymore."

"I said I was sorry. Shish kebab."

"Did you just say 'shish kebab'?"

"I said it instead of 'sheesh.'"

"Why didn't you just say 'sheesh'?"

"If everyone thought that way, we wouldn't have many words to use in conversation."

"You're distracting me."

"You're the one who asked me the question! Shish kebab!"

Drew sighed, making it clear we weren't having a fun conversation. He went on.

"And were they really ever your friends?" he asked. "You thought they liked you because you hung out in detention together, but they just wanted to be on the good side of the Sweet brothers, and look what it got you. You weren't invited to Angie's party, just like me, and now they've turned on you, just like that. I would've never turned on you like that, Peter."

I groaned.

"You're right, Drew," I said. "I've really messed things up. They're going to tell the principal I'm the thief Monday if

I can't catch the real thief and return their items. And it totally looks like I am the thief—I stole those chemicals from science class, and I am a magician . . . I need your help. I don't care about the loser experiment—I'm in worse trouble than that."

He stared at his shoes.

"You shouldn't have accused me of being the thief."

"I know, but I'm really confused right now," I said. "Plus, you're the one who broke us up and made up this experiment in the first place. I just want things to go back to how they used to."

"It can never be just like it used to," Drew said. I didn't say anything. He looked up at me. "But what choice do we have? Tell me how we're going to catch the real thief."

I shook my head.

"I'm done screwing things up for us," I replied. "We're going to have to figure this one out together."

"It's because I'm good at thinking outside the box, huh?"

"You're way better than I am, at this point."

"Let's put our thinking caps on and head up to Corbett Canyon," he shouted.

"Okay, but promise me you'll never use the phrase 'thinking caps' again for the rest of your life, okay? It's *so* fifth grade."

We climbed up into Corbett Canyon, and when I sat on

the floor I felt something hard stick into my back. I reached behind me and pulled out Hugh's yearbook.

"Check it out," I said, tossing it to Drew.

"He let you borrow it?"

"Not exactly," I said. "I'll return it later, he won't even know it was missing."

"Are you sure you're not the thief?" Drew asked.

"Just be careful with the pages."

"What's this?" he asked when he got to the Last Will and Testament section. I explained it to him. He stared at the wall for a minute. Then he started nodding to himself as if he was hearing invisible music. "We can use this."

He stared at me. A lightbulb started flickering inside my brain, but I couldn't quite grasp what Drew was getting at, so it kinda just flickered on and off in that way basement lightbulbs do that make it seem even scarier than not having any light at all.

"Don't you see, all we have to do is make up a phony thief to get you off the hook! The thief is going to tease everyone on the Lost-and-Found Forum message board tonight about how nobody can catch him. Then we'll have a way to communicate with him."

"How do you know this already?" I asked him, the hairs on the back of my neck standing up. "Are you sure *you're* not the thief?"

"You're not following me," he said. "Think about it—we're popular in other towns, remember?"

"But we're not, Drew." I sighed. "You don't really need me to go over that with you again, do you? And what does that have to do with anything?"

"Sure we are—we're friends with make-believe kids from Halliston, Peter!"

The lightbulb in my brain finally flickered on for good, and I smiled. But then,

"But they could just accuse me of making up the fake thief, and we'd be nowhere," I pointed out.

"You're right," he admitted, thinking about it for a few seconds. "Well, I guess you guys will have to try to catch the thief, then."

"Now you're not making sense again."

"No, hear me out—you and the detention club reach out to the fake thief, which is actually us, but they won't know that. You guys pose as a lonely, angry student on the yearbook committee who actually supports what the thief's doing. Make it sound like you consider the thief a modern-day Robin Hood or something, and that you hate everyone, too, so you offer to help the thief out by giving the thief an advance copy of this year's Last Will and Testament. That would be kinda like the holy grail for the thief, don't you think?"

"And then what?"

"Then you set a trap to catch the thief near the hill at school, and I'll show up disguised as the thief, and then you'll chase me and we'll lose them—and you can just say the thief escaped, and they'll have to believe that the thief isn't you!"

I frowned.

"But it's risky. It hinges on us being able to get distance from the others. What if they catch you, first?"

Drew beamed at me.

"That's why we'll set the trap next to the hill so we can use our land-skiing abilities to lose them. Nobody's faster than us, right?"

"You. Are. A. Genius," I said.

"I have my moments," Drew said, turning away from me and sort of staring up at the ceiling with a dreamy look on his face. After five seconds I got really bored waiting for him to stop feeling so thrilled with himself. Finally, he looked over at me and blushed. "The moment ended already, huh?"

I put a hand on his shoulder.

"It's one thing to have a moment, but it's even cooler to know exactly how long those moments last."

"But I don't get them very often."

"No, it's not a big deal, I'm just saying. . . ."

"Well, let's get to work on the thief's message, then," he said.

twenty-five

EVERYONE WAS BUZZING ABOUT THE thief the next morning, and the lobby sounded like a beehive. "It's official," a seventh grader said to Drew. "The thief wrote the school a message!"

"What are you talking about?" Drew replied, trying to seem completely clueless, but he overdid it and came off more like he was just coming out of a coma.

"I printed it out in computer lab, check it out," the kid said, handing Drew a rumpled piece of paper. Drew kept a straight face as he showed me the message we'd composed the night before.

To My Classmates at Fenwick Middle School
Reply to: "The Thief" <thethief123@ballyhoo.com>

Subject: hey

I'm just writing to inform you that you have not misplaced your favorite possessions—I've stolen them! And I won't stop until I've stolen everyone's favorite possessions. Because you deserve it.

Sincerely,
The Thief of Fenwick Middle

The Sweet brothers and Trent came over to us.

"What do you think you're doing, writing the school like that?" Hugh asked me.

"I told you, I'm not the thief," I replied.

I couldn't help but blush even though I wasn't the real thief, I was merely posing as him to clear my name . . . it was getting confusing for me to keep track of it all at this point.

"This doesn't change things," Trent said. "Whether this message was from you or not, if you don't catch the thief or return my basketball, we're turning you in on Monday."

"And my hat," Hank added.

"I have a plan for catching the thief," I said, but they walked away. I called out to them, "I'll explain it in detention!"

"Don't worry, this'll work," Drew said, nudging my elbow.

"Just make sure you're sitting at your computer after school so you can respond as the thief like we'd planned."

"No more talking about it at school," he suggested. "Just to make sure no one figures out we're behind this."

"That's a good idea," I agreed.

Drew frowned.

"I said no more talking!"

"I was just agreeing with the plan," I said.

"Now you're talking again."

"So are you!"

"What part of 'no more talking' do you not understand?"

I sighed.

"Okay," I said. "From this moment on, no more talking."

Drew's face turned red after a few seconds, and finally he leaned over and whispered in a kid's ear. The kid turned to me and said, "Drew says, see you in homeroom."

"Tell Drew I said, 'Not if I see you first,'" I instructed him.

"You guys are weird," the kid said, and walked away.

Apparently, it's really hard for me and Drew to stop talking to each other.

At detention that afternoon I finally explained my plan to catch the thief.

"Personally, I still think you're the thief, but if you aren't and this message is legit, I can see why the thief would want it—the Last Will and Testament's basically a shopping list for the thief," Trent admitted.

"But Peter's the thief!" Donnie cried.

"Look, what choice do you have but to believe me?" I said calmly. "You want your things back by Monday, right? If I'm telling the truth, then I'm going to need your help to catch the real thief."

"I vote Peter back in as leader of the investigation," Hugh said, crossing his arms.

Everyone looked at Donnie. His brow was furrowed. Then he looked at me.

"This might just work," he admitted. "If you really aren't the thief."

"So what now?" Hank asked me.

"The first step is we have to make contact with the thief," I continued. "I've composed a letter to set the bait, but I need someone to set up a fake email address so we can communicate privately with him without the feds busting us, since our first message is going to be on the Lost-and-Found Forum."

"I'm on it," Donnie replied, eager to have a major role in the hunt.

When the late bell rang, we ran outside and took the late

bus over to Sally's house. Donnie sat down at her desk and set up a phony Guggle email address on her laptop while I took out the letter to the thief that I'd written earlier. Sally then typed up the message, since it was her computer and she wanted to have a role, too. When she was done, she called us over.

From: <TDC@guggle.com>
To: "The Thief" <thethief123@ballyhoo.com>
Subject: Re: hey

Dear Thief,

I know it seems like everyone at Fenwick Middle wants your head on a platter, but not everyone feels that way. Personally I think it's great that you're stealing from these jerks, and I want to help. I'm too scared to steal things myself, but I thought of a way I could help you. I have in my possession this year's Last Will and Testament. It lists every eighth grader's most prized possession, and as you know, the yearbook doesn't come out till the end of the school year. I'd be willing to give it to you now. It would make me feel like I'm getting my revenge, too. If you're interested, reply and we can set up a time and place to meet.

Sincerely,

A friend

"What do you guys think?" she asked.

"It's not bad," Trent said. "We'll get the thief to meet us somewhere, and then we'll ambush him!"

"That's *if* the thief isn't Peter," Donnie reminded everyone.

"Hit send already, Shakespeare," Hank said, and Sally clicked the mouse.

"Actually, she's more like Shakespeare's typist, while I'm the real Shakespeare," I clarified, but they ignored me.

"Now what?" she asked.

"I guess we wait," I said.

Donnie stared at me.

"You know, if you *are* the thief, we're not going to get a reply right now, we'll just get one later when you're alone and can write back, so it won't prove anything."

"Yes, that would be the case if I actually was the thief, but I'm telling you I'm not," I said, stalling by talking really slowly. Fortunately, Drew was on top of his game back home, and a moment later Sally's computer beeped. Everyone looked shocked.

"I guess that proves it," Trent said to Donnie. They both looked a little disappointed, actually.

From: "The Thief" <*thethief123@ballyhoo.com*>
To: <*TDC@guggle.com*>

232

Subject: Re: hey

You say you are a friend, but how can I know for sure? You could be a student hoping to catch me. It doesn't matter, though, because I'm a really cautious person, and I never make mistakes, and I don't need what it is you are offering because I am all knowing. But you happen to catch me in a moment where I want to help you find happiness, too, so I will let you help me, under strict conditions.

We will meet on Saturday, at 4:00 p.m., in the middle of the soccer field at school. I will be checking the surrounding area to make sure you didn't bring anyone w/ you. When I feel the coast is clear, I will make my presence known. You will then hold up the Last Will and Testament, to prove you have it. You will then place it on the ground. You will then start walking off the field. Do not turn around as you walk away. Then you will have your revenge.

Sincerely,

The Thief of Fenwick Middle

I watched everyone read the email in silence, their faces lit up blue by the computer screen. They looked excited, and a little bit scared—which seemed like a good thing, because that meant they believed it.

"Can we all make it on Saturday?" Hugh asked.

Everyone nodded.

"I can't wait for the hunt—we're going to catch the thief and be heroes!" Hank shouted, and I started high-fiving with everyone before remembering the real situation. I turned away from them and sighed. I didn't like having to juggle all these lies; it was hard to keep track of them all at this point. I couldn't wait for it to all be over so I could go to T.A.G. during the week and to Angie's parties on weekends.

I couldn't eat anything at dinner that night because I felt too antsy about the hunt. If Drew got caught, we'd both be in trouble, and it would totally look like we really were the thief even though we weren't.

"Why are you so fidgety?" Sunny asked.

"No reason," I said quickly. "I'm just hyper, I guess, from hanging out with Trent and Sally. They, um, gave me a lot of candy."

"Congratulations," she said softly.

Seeing her look jealous didn't make me feel good like I'd thought it would. Maybe it was because I knew that this tiny victory was based on my lie that things were great with the detention club, but usually that doesn't stop me.

"Why aren't you eating anything?" Mom asked.

"I'm not hungry," Sunny and I said at the same time.

"She was talking to me," I explained, playing with my peas.

"Actually, I was talking to your sister," Mom said.

I looked at Sunny. Her face was kinda pale.

"You look sick," I noted. "No, I don't mean lookswise, I mean you really look like you're sick."

"He's right," Dad said. "Do you have a fever?"

"I just have a lot of work to do, may I be excused?" she asked.

Dad nodded, and she left the table. He looked over at my untouched plate and nodded at me. "And you shouldn't be eating candy before dinner, haven't we told you before that it ruins your appetite?"

"I assumed it was a theory you'd never actually tested out, since you've never kept sweets inside our house."

"Do you have a bellyache?" Mom asked.

"No, I just have a lot of work to do, too," I said. I wasn't thinking about my regular schoolwork that I regularly wasn't doing, but the inventors' fair. That was another reason I couldn't wait for the hunt to be behind us—my brain was too nervous to think about anything else, which meant I couldn't work on my inventions at night, either.

She smiled. "We'll keep your plate in the microwave and

235

you can eat after you do some work," she said, and I got up from the table.

"I'm glad you're buckling down with your studies like this, Son," said Dad.

"Right," I said, not looking at him.

twenty-six

I T WAS CLOUDY ON SATURDAY when the Detention Club met up as planned behind the school. The Sweet brothers were wearing those bank-robber ski hats that cover the entire face except for holes for eyes and the nose. They looked pretty intimidating.

"This is it," I shouted, and they shushed me. "Oh, right. Good call."

"Let's go," Sally said. "It's almost time."

"Hold on, I brought protection," Trent said, unzipping a big red bag. He pulled out a bunch of hockey sticks and passed them around.

"We're not going to hurt the thief, and we don't need those, we outnumber him six to one," I pointed out.

"It's just for intimidation," Trent explained.

"I'm not sure I could hit the thief with a hockey stick, if it ever came to it," Sally said, staring at her hockey stick.

"Where's mine?" I asked.

"You're going to be out in the soccer field, so you can't have a hockey stick on you," Trent explained.

"Why do I have to be the drop-off guy?"

"You're the littlest."

I shivered because it was so cold out, and that made me seem legitimately scared.

"Don't worry, we'll protect you," Hank said, clapping me on the back.

It made me feel warm inside to hear that.

"Let's go, we have to make sure we hide before the thief gets there," Donnie said, and we made our way over to the woods next to the soccer field.

Trent handed me a piece of paper. Typed across the page a dozen times, it read:

Ha ha, you've just been caught!

"I can't wait to see the look on his face," Sally said.

I stared out at the soccer field. A heavy wind rolled across the field, driving up the powdery top layer of cracked dirt on the ground into a poofy cloud.

"You're going to do fine," Trent said. "You just have to be

the bait, and leave the rest to us."

Trent stepped behind a bush and crouched down, and I took a deep breath and stepped out onto the field. My ears were freezing and my feet felt heavy, but I trudged out to the center of the field. I turned and faced the woods. I looked for everyone, and even though I wanted Drew to be able to spot them for his own safety, I was kind of disappointed at how easy they were to spot. Sally had her arms sticking out from a tree, pretending they were branches, but she was shivering wildly so the tree looked alive. Donnie was holding out his hockey stick as if it was a tree limb, but there was shiny silver duct tape wrapped around the handle.

It was getting darker by the minute. All the houses across the road from the school had their lights on already. One house had a Halloween display in the yard—some plastic ghosts hanging from branches and a lit-up inflatable pumpkin by the front door. I felt something hit my nose. I stuck out my tongue and waited for a raindrop to land on it, but it was barely sprinkling. "There he is, get him!" Hugh suddenly shouted, and I practically bit my tongue off. There was a dark figure standing at the edge of the soccer field. It was Drew! He was wearing a hoodie to hide his face, which I thought was really clever.

Suddenly the Detention Club hollered as they charged out of the woods at the thief, waving their hockey sticks like flyswatters as they raced past me. Drew jumped nearly three feet off the ground. It looked like a dogfight from World War I or something, Drew running in circles as they gave chase. He broke for the woods, and the Detention Club raced after him.

"Don't let him escape!" Donnie shouted at me.

I intentionally slipped so Drew could get by me, before I got up and chased after him. Just as we'd hoped, our land-skiing abilities helped us pull away from the pack as we hurtled down the hill. I could hear the rest of the Detention Club shouting behind me, and it sounded like they'd stopped running. I glanced back and saw Donnie and Sally dragging their heavy hockey sticks on the ground.

"Get him, Pete!" Hank shouted. He was huffing and puffing.

I focused on my land-skiing technique, weaving expertly around the trees.

"You're gaining on him!" Trent shouted.

"Go, Peter!" Sally's fading voice called out to me.

I smiled to myself—I was amazing everyone with my land-skiing! I could hear breaking branches, and the occasional "Oof" behind me as the Detention Club struggled to catch up to us. I made a mental note to teach them how to land-ski in the future.

By the time we reached the bottom of the hill, I was now

an arm's length away from Drew, and I made a dramatic lunge for him, grabbing hold of the hood before I let it tug out of my hand. I let myself tumble in a heap on the leafy floor and smiled as Drew kept booking it around the corner. A moment later the others crashed through the line of branches into the clearing, and I forced myself to stop giggling.

"Where is he?" Donnie shouted.

Sally had her hockey stick held out in front of her as she charged forward and nearly jabbed me point-blank in the face.

"What happened, Peter? You were right on top of him!" Trent said.

"The thief got away," I said quickly, pretending to breathe heavily even though land-skiing, if you have good form like I do, doesn't really tire you out all that much.

At this point everyone started spazzing out and slamming their hockey sticks against trees because they were so upset. Sally hit hers on a tree near me and I got doused with rainwater.

"Could you stop doing that, please?" I asked her, but she ignored me, and kept swinging away at the trunk.

"I can't believe we lost the thief," Hugh said.

"And the thief has seen us all, so now he'll target us more," Trent added.

"We're all in serious danger!" Donnie said, kinda wigging out.

"I can't believe we didn't catch the thief," Sally said. "After all this work! You have all these complicated plans, Peter, and they always fall through."

"But we've gotten closer," I said.

"No, you're bad luck," Sally said, then looked down at her feet and groaned. "And now I've ruined my white shoes!"

"Okay, so you're definitely not the thief, but your ideas for catching the real thief stink," Donnie said to me. "No more wasting our time listening to your stupid ideas."

Even though this was different from when Drew had said it, given that I'd bungled this plan on purpose, it still hurt. I should have felt happy that things had worked out, but I recognized the expression on everyone's faces—it was the look they used to give me before all of this started. I was merely back to square one.

They left me standing there.

I watched them disappear up the hill. When they were the size of ants, I finally turned around and headed over to Brook Street. I was supposed to stop at Drew's to tell him how things went, but instead I headed straight home. My parents and Sunny were waiting for me in the kitchen. Sunny had a big grin on her face, which I knew from experience meant something really bad was about to happen to me, and I cringed. Dad pointed at the seat in front of him. "Sit." What now, I wondered?

On the table were five pieces of paper. Each one was for a different class, but they all said pretty much the same thing—I was failing all my classes. Here's what one of them looked like:

Fenwick Middle School First-Semester Progress Reports

Dear Mr. and Mrs. Lee:

This is to inform you that Peter Lee is currently failing Math Class. His quiz average is 62 percent and his test average is 57 percent.

Teacher: Mrs. Ryder_____

Parent's Signature:_____

"What have you been doing during study time?" Mom asked.

"I d'no," I said.

She threw her hands up in the air and went upstairs. Dad took his glasses off and rubbed his eyes. "Your mother is very upset—we're both very upset. When you got that fourteen percent on the quiz, we thought it was just a one-time thing—maybe you overslept that day—but to see that you're failing *all* of your classes? This is just the start of middle school! What is going wrong? Why are you getting such bad grades?"

"I've been doing a new kind of studying that's eventually going to revolutionize the way we study. I can't take notes as fast as everyone else, so I've been taking digital pictures of the blackboards and studying them before tests. In theory it's so much faster."

"What on earth are you talking about?"

"I'll show you," I said, and led him up to the office. I opened up the folder on the screen and showed him the pics. That they were so meticulously organized kinda felt impressive, and for a second I was expecting to get congratulated for how clever I was. I looked up at him and he was shaking his head. "The only problem is your camera's not nice enough, so I couldn't actually read the notes. See? It's not my fault I have bad grades—you need a newer camera."

"You can't take shortcuts like this," he said. "Why didn't you come to us if you had problems?"

"I don't know."

"Maybe this is our fault," Dad said.

"I appreciate your having an open mind about this," I said quickly. "Um, can I go now?"

"Sit down!" he snapped. He shook his head. "I suppose you're under a lot of pressure. We want you to do as well as

Sunny, but your sister does awfully well. Is that hard for you?"

I blushed.

"No, I'm just different from her."

"But you're a bright boy, you're just as bright as she is," he said. "Let me see your notebooks."

We went to my bedroom. I didn't want him to see the notebooks, because I knew there wasn't really anything in them. I prayed as he looked through them that some magical elf had filled them up with good notes while I was sleeping the night before. Of course I didn't really believe it was possible, but that didn't stop me from praying. "Please help me, magical elf," I whispered, but when Dad opened the notebooks they were all mostly empty.

"You haven't taken notes all semester!" he wailed.

"Let's not forget that a big reason for that is because I thought you had a halfway decent digital camera. And frankly, I'm a little disappointed that you aren't noticing that I didn't get a progress report from T.A.G. class," I said, and he groaned. "Relax, Pops, here—look at this one."

I handed over my inventor's notebook. He flipped through the pages and I was positive that seeing how the thing was practically full would make him feel a little less frustrated. Instead he waved the notebook at me.

"This is the problem," he said. "You've been daydreaming all semester!"

"Dad, I know it's hard to believe because it hasn't happened yet, but I'm going to be a major inventor someday," I said.

"You aren't responsible enough to be in that class right now," he said, and I gulped. "Until you bring your grades up, you can't participate in T.A.G. class."

"I already haven't even gone in a month because of detention," I pointed out. "I'm going to have to make my prototype without Ms. Schoonmaker's help!"

"I mean you can't waste any more time working on your inventions—you can't participate in that inventors' fair, either."

My stomach shriveled into itself.

"But—"

"No buts about it. Not anymore. I need you to buckle down and do well in school. Maybe in the spring you can rejoin the T.A.G. program," he said. At this point Sunny and Mom were standing in the doorway. "If your sister can find time to study hard and still work on her inventions, so can you. Right, Sunny?"

"Right," she said quietly. Strangely, she didn't have that evil smile on her face and almost looked like she felt bad for me, even.

After Dad left, I closed my bedroom door. I very quietly picked up the phone and called Drew. I explained what had just happened "Maybe it's finally time we consider running away," I said.

Drew didn't say anything for a couple of seconds.

"What you need to do is win that inventors' fair on Tuesday," he finally said.

"Didn't you hear what I just said? My parents said I can't do it anymore until I pull my grades up."

"Look, your parents are all about results, right? Sunny wins all those medals and plaques and the talent show every year—you just need to win the inventors' fair to get back in their good graces. But also by winning you'll probably get a free pass for the semester since they can't flunk out the school's representative for the National Young Inventors' Competition, and on top of that we'll finally become the kings of the school again. Do you see? By winning the fair, you can kill three birds with one stone, like you say."

"It's two, but it's not possible anyway—I haven't been able to go to T.A.G. class in a month, remember? I don't even have a prototype prepared."

"You can do it, Peter," he said. "And I'll help you—together we can come up with the winning entry. If we're both thinking outside the box, we'll set a record for being the furthest away from one, probably."

"I don't know if it's possible," I said, but the more I thought about it, the more I realized Drew was right. What choice did we have at this point? Besides, Dad had pounded into my head for years how important it is to stick to your strengths. Like when Mom would tell him to do the dishes for a change, he'd say, "We have to stick to our strengths, honey. Mine's mowing the lawn." My strength, I remembered, was being an inventor. Since Drew's not a mind reader, he didn't know that I'd just come to this conclusion and figured I still needed convincing.

"Remember what you told me?" he said. "Alexander Graham Bell took a thousand tries before he finally invented the microwave."

"It was Edison, and he invented the lightbulb," I corrected him.

"Whatever," he replied. "The point is, if he can do it, so can you!"

"You mean us," I said.

"Right—so can us!"

"Well now, that's just bad English," I pointed out.

"How would you know—you're failing English, aren't you?"

"Touché."

twenty-seven

O N SUNDAY DREW AND I hung out in Corbett Canyon trying to choose an invention from my inventor's notebook to take to the prototype stage. The problem was that the rest of my ideas for inventions were really advanced and complex, and in order to build a decent prototype we'd need a lot of seed money. "I can't believe I have a whole notebook full of ideas and none of them are doable," I said, shaking my head. "Maybe I'm not a great inventor like we thought."

"We're just going to have to come up with something new," Drew said.

"We only have two days—it's hopeless, Drew."

He patted me on the back.

"You have to be more positive!" he said. "Look, we need

to come up with an invention that's either fun or helps the environment—or, if we're lucky, both—so let's think about it. What do people do for fun?"

"Listen to music? Play video games? Sports?"

Drew sat there for a minute, thinking really hard. His smile disappeared as the seconds ticked by.

"Are you thinking outside the box, Drew?"

"Actually, it feels like the opposite," he said, wincing. "Just thinking about this stuff makes me feel like I'm in the middle of space, like when you shut your eyes and stare at the universe in your head."

"You can see the universe, too?" I asked. "I thought I was the only one . . . anyway, we don't have the computer-programming skills to make a video game, and we don't play instruments or sports. We lasted only one season in youth soccer because we kept losing our cleats at the park, remember?"

"That's because cleats are stupid—you have to take them off and change into normal shoes in order to walk across the parking lot." Drew's eyes widened as he said this. "Okay, so what if we were to figure out a way to make it so you can wear cleats like normal shoes off the playing field, so you don't have to forget them on the sidelines every weekend?"

I felt a tingling sensation in my brain, which was either a good thing or a sign that I had a brain tumor. "It's the same with ice skates," I said, nodding. "Remember when you refused to take yours off that one time and tried to walk to the car in them, and you fell and cut your leg on the blade?"

"Don't remind me," he said, rubbing his left thigh as if it still hurt.

"But it's like all sports shoes—you can only use them for playing sports—what a scam."

"You're right! Like when my dad used to take me golfing, he had to take his golf shoes off before we drove home, because of the spikes."

"I'm feelin' you, I hear you barking. And so this would be environmental because people wouldn't need extra pairs of shoes, they could just wear their sports shoes all over the place," I said.

"Yeah, totally, and think about it, when soccer shoes wear out, the leather on top is still in good condition, it's just that the studs on the bottom wear out. What a waste of leather."

"Yes, yes," I said, feeding off his genius. "We could save millions of cows from getting killed for their leather!"

"Not to mention saving the lives of all those hockey players and figure skaters who die every year cutting themselves with their own shoes! How many figure skaters do you think die every year from cutting themselves with their own skates?"

"You'd have to guess at least ten thousand," I said, scratching my chin. "Maybe more, worldwide."

Drew frowned.

"The thing is, even though I've never actually met one, I've always felt like I wouldn't like a figure skater in person," he said.

"I know what you mean, but we can't play God," I warned him. "If we have the knowledge to save lives, we have no choice but to use it."

"No, you're totally right," he replied. "I just would hate it if we met one someday and they were really snobby to us, though."

"Well, that just means we're better people than all figure skaters, then," I said, and he agreed.

We'd never brainstormed together like this, and it kinda made me feel like I was out of breath or something. Drew must have been thinking the same thing, because he said, "Do you have any idea how smart we are when we put our heads together? Why didn't we start doing this sooner?"

"It's scary, actually," I said. "We should build a time machine or something."

"One invention at a time, buddy," he said, but I could tell by the look in his eyes that he was excited about building a time machine, too.

"I can't believe we just invented this!" I shouted.

We jumped up and down for a minute, celebrating. Only since we were in Corbett Canyon and the ceiling was so low, we had to kind of duck as we jumped, which made me feel like a kangaroo, but it still felt pretty fun.

"Okay, that's probably enough," I said, and we sat back down on the floor.

"So how do we do it?" Drew finally asked.

"What you do is step into figure skates that have the invention stuck onto the bottom of it so it's like wearing regular soles."

"Boom," he said. "But wait—wouldn't the blade just stick through the sole?"

"I guess we'd have to fill the bottom of the replacement sole with some kind of high-tech gooey material that the spikes could sink into and stay in place . . . Silly Putty?"

"Too mushy, wouldn't hold the cleats," Drew said. A second later his eyes lit up. "I know what we can use!"

We rode our bikes over to Stop & Shop, and I had no idea what Drew was doing, but when he headed over to the florist inside the grocery store, it made perfect sense—that green foamy stuff they use to stick flowers into for bouquets! Luckily, a different lady was working the register, so she didn't recognize us from back when we'd destroyed all their inventory after picking up fake Emma's birthday cake, and she didn't even charge us; in fact, she gave us a dozen foamy green cubes for free in a plastic bag.

After detention on Monday I ran straight to Corbett Canyon, where Drew and I gathered up his old ice skates and a pair of his dad's old golf shoes that he'd left behind when he moved out. We glued a foamy cube onto the bottoms, and voilà, we had our prototype! "This was surprisingly easy," I noted. "Usually that's a bad sign with us."

"Not this time," Drew said. "I think we hit pay dirt with this one, I really do."

"Should we test it out a few times to make sure it works?" I asked.

Drew looked at me with big eyes, and I knew he was thinking what I was thinking. We really wanted to poke holes in the foamy cubes for fun.

"But if we do that, we won't have enough to test out the prototype," Drew said.

I stared at the pile of foamy green cubes in the corner. They looked so inviting.

"I'm pretty sure the prototype will work fine, how about you?"

A second later we raced over to the foamy cubes and started poking holes in them and giggling like crazy.

"This is even funner than playing with bubble wrap," Drew said.

"Now *that's* an invention," I agreed.

twenty-eight

THE INVENTORS' FAIR WAS SCHEDULED for seventh period the next day. Everyone in T.A.G. got to skip sixth period to set up their inventions. I got to the gym after lunch and saw that decorations had already been put up all over the place. In the center of the basketball court, facing the bleachers, was a raised platform with a podium on it. Behind the podium was a line of chairs for the presenters, and already most of the members were setting up their inventions. It was my first time seeing their prototypes, and I felt nervous at first because they all looked kinda interesting. Angie had what looked like a black stick with a plastic claw attached to the end. Carson had a Styrofoam box that he was putting a small sheet over to hide it. What was in that Styrofoam box? Graham was sitting in his chair holding what looked like a normal toothbrush. Maybe he was planning on brushing his teeth right before the assembly?

I took the corner seat and draped a blanket over it so they wouldn't see my project. Ms. Schoonmaker was checking on all of us, sipping her tiny cup of espresso, and it amazed me that her little cup could make the entire gym reek like a Starbucks. "That looks interesting, Carson, though you might want to go over the title on your poster one more time with the marker so everyone can see it," she said. "How's your setup going, Peter?"

She peeked at my prototype and her eyes grew wide.

"Now that looks very interesting. Care to offer any hint as to what it is?"

"You'll know soon enough," I said.

"I'm proud of you—you showed real initiative working on your prototype even though you had to miss some classes. Just presenting at all today is an accomplishment."

"Well, I'm shooting for better than that," I said, and she patted me on the head. Usually I hate it when adults do that because it makes me feel like a pony, but this time I kinda enjoyed it.

"Sunny, are you ready? Sunny?" Ms. Schoonmaker asked. I looked over and saw that my sister was sitting in her seat, and her face was bright red. The yellow duffel bag in front of her was zipped shut. "Why haven't you taken out your prototype? We only have a few minutes before it starts."

"I don't have one," Sunny said softly.

Everyone's jaws dropped.

"What do you mean? You've been working on it all semester," Ms. Schoonmaker said.

"I switched at the last minute because my main idea wasn't working, but I couldn't get it done in time." She stared at the floor, and I noticed the bags under her eyes that made her look ancient, like she was twenty or something.

"Well, maybe you could still present what you have so far. Let's see it," Ms. Schoonmaker said, reaching for the duffel bag.

"No!" Sunny pulled the bag away from her. "I'm not presenting this afternoon."

Ms. Schoonmaker frowned at her.

"I'm very disappointed to hear this. You should have told me earlier. We could have helped you finish your project on time."

"Can I just turn something in by the end of the week?"

"For a grade, yes, but I'm afraid the selection process ends today. You knew that already, though. This is so unlike you."

Sunny's face turned redder.

"I don't care!" she suddenly burst out, picking up the duffel bag and running for the double doors. Ms. Schoonmaker called after her, but she was gone. She turned to us.

"Okay, the rest of you have your prototypes ready, and I expect you to do your best presenting them. Good luck, everybody!"

I couldn't believe it. I would have never guessed in a million years that my sister would crack under pressure like this. I didn't feel bad for her, though, because a second later it dawned on me that—with my main competition out of the way—I now really did have a chance to win this thing! The bell rang for seventh period, and we sat down in our seats. I could hear the pounding of footsteps and shouts and hollers outside, and a minute later the entire student body spilled in through the double doors and raced past us to the bleachers. It took a while for everyone to settle down before Ms. Schoonmaker went up to the podium and spoke into the microphone.

"Welcome, students! I'm pleased to announce the start of the first-ever Fenwick Middle School Inventors' Fair. This afternoon you will be shown several inventions from your peers in The Academically Gifted program, from which one winner will be chosen by our judges at the end to represent our school next spring at the National Young Inventors' Competition. First up is . . . Angie Westphals!"

I was relieved that she didn't start with me. Now I would be going last. The students were already murmuring about

Sunny's absence, whispering her name so much that it sounded like a bleacher full of snakes. They were stunned that for the first time in two years she wouldn't be in the running to win an official school competition. I pictured her yellow duffel bag. It had been full when she hoisted it up and raced out of the gym a few minutes earlier—what was her unfinished invention?

"Peter, stop daydreaming and pay attention!" Ms. Schoonmaker whispered in my ear from behind, and I almost passed out from the espresso smell.

Angie's invention turned out to be a sugar-cube dispenser for her horse, so she could give it a treat midride. Aside from Sally and the rest of the equestrian girls, the audience didn't seem all that interested. "One down, five to go," I whispered to myself as the students politely applauded at the end of her presentation.

Next up was Carson. It turned out his invention wasn't in the Styrofoam box—it *was* the Styrofoam box. All he did was stick a freeze pack in it, along with a sandwich, a juice box, some chips, and a Snickers bar. He explained that Styrofoam's really bad for the environment and doesn't decompose, and this way we could reuse it rather than crowd landfills with the stuff, and on top of this Styrofoam is really good at keeping things cool. Big woop.

"No more soggy sandwiches, no more warm drinks, no

more melted chocolate bars. The Carsonator not only saves the environment by recycling Styrofoam, but it keeps your meals the way they ought to be," he said, and started noisily munching on the food samples. "Mmm, the lettuce in my sandwich is so crisp. Oooh, I'm getting freezer burn sipping this juice box. Yow—I almost chipped a tooth biting into my frozen Snickers bar!"

"Give me a break," I muttered, and Ms. Schoonmaker glared at me.

When Carson was finished, everyone in the stands clapped a little louder than they had for Angie, who blushed—apparently she'd thought her horse claw was going to be sweeping the nation someday. I looked over at Ms. Schoonmaker and the judges—surely they'd deduct points given the fact that all Carson had done was tape two pieces of Styrofoam together.

The other inventions weren't even as good as that one, believe it or not. Leigh had cut out two sides of a milk carton, stapled a garbage bag to one end, and fastened a broom handle to the top. "It's called the Leaf Picker Upper," she said. "This way you can rake leaves and they automatically go in the trash bag, so you have one less step to do!"

I looked over at the judges and they were scribbling notes, probably pointing out that basically Leigh's invention was promoting obesity, because people would get fatter by not having to do that extra step when raking the yard. I don't even remember Courtney's or Sam's invention, and the worst was easily Graham's. Like Carson, he didn't even invent anything, really. According to him, his toothbrush was a toothbrush for . . . toothbrushes! He called it the T2, which you'd use to clean your toothbrush after you brush your teeth. "Now you don't have to go into the bathroom, wanting to clean your teeth, and find that your toothbrush has a speck of old chicken in the bristles from your last meal."

"Gross," someone in the audience shouted.

"And, um, so now your toothbrushes will last longer, because dentists say that it's important to not only take care of your teeth, but also, um, your toothbrushes. . . ." Graham's voice trailed off, and to be honest, I kinda felt bad for him.

I couldn't believe how lame these inventions were—all semester these kids had been working so hard on them, and this was the best they had to offer? I was excited to finally give my presentation. It had come down to this. This was my moment, my chance to win over my classmates, my chance to guarantee that I wouldn't get kicked out of T.A.G., and on top of that I'd defeated Sunny just by even participating, since she'd already quit! But I kind of wished she was there to see it—I wanted to watch the look on her face when I unveiled what me and Drew had decided to call Safe Soles. Finally, for once she'd have to admit (at least to herself) that I was actually better at something than her.

"And now, last but not least, we have Peter Lee," Ms. Schoonmaker announced. She was sipping her espresso and didn't seem as excited about the competition as she had at the start, thanks to Graham's T2. Well, all that was about to change, I thought. I stood up and carried my bag up to the podium.

"Good afternoon, everybody. . . . Um, what I've done is fix the problem that all athletes have—how many of you hate having to take your ice skates or soccer cleats or golf shoes off before you walk to your parents' car?"

Almost everyone raised their hands! As I whipped off the blanket, everyone leaned forward to get a look. I glanced over at the judges, who they were craning their necks trying to see my prototype.

"I call them Safe Soles, and what you do is simply step into them after you play your sports. That way you can walk normally in your hockey skates or soccer cleats the rest of the day. You can ride your bike in your golf shoes, walk the dog in your ice skates, go ballroom dancing in your soccer cleats, with no risk of accidentally killing yourself and others!"

Students oohed and aahed, and even Ms. Schoonmaker was smiling!

"Now for a demonstration—my assistant Drew will show you how it works," I said, and Drew climbed out of the stands and joined me up on the platform. I placed the Safe Soles by his feet as he put on his ice skates. Drew then stepped into the foamy replacement soles and everyone cheered! The foam was too weak, though, so basically Drew had to balance on his skates and walk real gingerly so the soles didn't fall off. Luckily the blades had dug into the actual soles a little and they stayed on, just barely. People stopped cheering—it looked like he was walking on stilts. I sat him down.

"Okay, that's the demonstration," I said quickly.

"You know, historically we've never been that good at demonstrations," Drew whispered as we listened to the scattered applause.

"Tell me about it," I whispered back. "Luckily everyone else's inventions were horrible."

Ms. Schoonmaker picked up the mic. "Okay, now I'll tally the votes from the judges, and we'll find out which young inventor is going to represent the school at the national competition this spring," she said.

I figured even though our demonstration hadn't gone perfectly, our Safe Soles were the obvious choice, but a minute later she returned to the podium and said, "And the winner is Carson Santiago, for his invention, the Carsonator!"

Everyone cheered, and then the bell rang, and students raced out of the gym as if it was on fire. Drew came over and put a hand on my shoulder.

"Are you upset?" he asked.

"Weirdly, no," I admitted.

I guess it happened so fast that I couldn't quite believe it at first. But then, as it started to sink in that we'd lost, I was surprised to find out that I wasn't feeling crushed. I sat there trying to figure out why I felt so calm about it. I mean, my fate had just been sealed in an instant—I was going to get kicked out of the T.A.G. program and probably flunk out of school altogether, I hadn't won the competition, I hadn't beaten Sunny even though she'd handed me the victory on a platter by not even participating, and me and Drew were going to be stuck being nobodies for the rest of our lives. And yet, it didn't really bother me like it should have. Fact is, instead of feeling bummed I'd lost, I couldn't stop wondering what the deal was with Sunny.

"Peter, may I speak with you for a moment?" Ms. Schoonmaker said. Drew motioned that he'd meet me over by the double doors. "The reason we didn't choose your invention, which was my personal favorite, was because the invention already exists, unfortunately."

"Really?"

"Mr. Tinsley said so, he has some for his golf shoes."

"But Styrofoam coolers already exist, too."

"It's more that he's recycling Styrofoam that the judges appreciated."

I sighed.

"I guess I'm not an inventor, after all."

"Quite the contrary!" she said. "You honestly invented something that already exists. This is proof that you're thinking creatively, that you have a real knack for it."

"So you're saying I was just born in the wrong century?" I asked, thinking about the time machine me and Drew were probably going to invent when we got older.

"I suppose. Anyway, good work. I'm proud that you were able to do this even though you missed some classes. Now get to your bus."

Drew and I didn't talk much on the walk home. He was probably debating land-skiing to New Hampshire again, while I couldn't stop picturing Sunny's duffel bag. I needed to see what her invention looked like. It was all I could think about. And so when he asked me if I wanted to hang out in Corbett Canyon until dinner, I shook my head.

"Maybe later," I said.

Sunny was already practicing the flute when I got home. I figured I could sneak into her bedroom upstairs and take a peek. She stopped playing but kept looking at her sheet music. "Did you win?" she asked.

"Carson won with a stupid Styrofoam thing. I'm in a bad mood, I think I need to be alone right now," I said, pretending to be really upset. It felt weird that I was having to pretend to be upset.

I went upstairs, stood outside my room, and slammed the door shut, then waited a few seconds for her flute to start playing again. Then I pushed her bedroom door open really quietly and snuck inside.

The yellow duffel bag was by the closet in the corner. I crept over to it. I took extra-soft steps because her bedroom was directly over the living room, so it ended up taking me almost five minutes to get to the corner. I bent over and slowly unzipped the duffel bag, and what I saw inside it made me gasp.

It was Sunny's invention, and it was incredible, way cooler than my Safe Soles! It was all chrome, with plastic buttons on it and some sort of round thing on it and a tray that came out and a big red power button. It even had a plug in the back. I touched the side of the machine and it was smooth, perfect. I sighed. Of course Sunny would end up making something so advanced that it looked futuristic, but why would she hide this from the inventors' competition, then? Surely this would have easily won, whatever it was.

"What are you doing here?"

Sunny was standing in the doorway. I scrambled to my feet.

"I just wanted to see your invention," I replied. "What is it?"

Her cheeks turned bright red for a second time that day.

"Get out of my room," she barked.

"What is that thing?" I asked her.

"Duh—it's Ms. Schoonmaker's espresso machine," she said.

"You made her a new espresso machine?"

She rolled her eyes.

"No, you moron, I stole it," she said. "I grabbed it during the Inventors' Fair."

I turned it over and saw that engraved on the bottom it read MADE IN CHINA.

"But you don't drink espresso," I said. "Why would you steal it?"

She sighed, then went over to the closet and slid the door open—and I couldn't believe what I was seeing. On the shelves were several cell phones, Trent's basketball, Carson's scientific calculator, a clump of barrettes, diaries, Sally's horseshoe key chain, a stack of books, a pair of ballet shoes, a Nalgene water bottle, a handful of cotton scarves . . .

"Because I'm the thief of Fenwick Middle," she said.

twenty-nine

I SAT DOWN ON THE BED. Actually I kinda fell back onto it. "But you can't be the thief," I said. "That's impossible. The thief is . . . why would you steal from everyone?"

She went over to the door and locked it even though our parents weren't home from work, and wouldn't be for at least another hour. She stared at the doorknob and said, "It's a long story."

I sat there on the bed, waiting for her to continue. She walked back over to the closet and picked up Carson's calculator. She pressed some buttons, but she was gazing out the window.

"I hate going to Fenwick Middle," she finally said. "Everyone's mean. In sixth grade I suddenly stopped getting invited to birthday parties or even just to hang out at a friend's house after school, so I started studying extra hard and got all A's, and I became president of all the clubs. My goal was to beat everyone in school at everything. I thought it would make me feel better, but it only made everyone hate me even more."

"But why would you steal things?"

"And then you started going to the school," she said, ignoring me. "And I didn't want you to see that nobody likes me. You and Mom and Dad think I'm the queen of the school, and I saw that you were making friends, and it made me mad. One day I saw Hank Sweet's hat sitting on his chair—he forgot it after lunch—and I don't know why, but I took it. I had my duffel bag with me, and I stuck it in there when nobody was looking.

"And the thing is, it made me feel happy in school for the first time ever. The next day Hank made fun of me before class, and for once it didn't make me mad, because I knew I had his favorite Notre Dame hat. And so I started stealing things from people and hiding them in the duffel bag, and it made going to school feel easier.

"So when kids are talking about an amazing birthday party they went to over the weekend, I don't feel as bad, because I have their barrettes and their diaries. It kind of gave me a sort of revenge for not being invited to the parties, I guess. But it felt gross, too, and I tried to stop, but I guess I got a little addicted to it."

"It's crazy you'd just carry that duffel bag around in school, didn't you care if you got caught?" I asked.

"Nobody suspected me because I'm Sunny Lee, the model student. I'm the straight arrow, the last person anyone would think was the thief."

I nodded. "It's like Dad always says—sometimes the hardest answer to find is the one staring right at you. He used to hide a bike reflector from me and Drew in plain sight, and we could never find it."

"Exactly."

"But wait, so why did you steal from Ms. Schoonmaker?"

"Because she got mad at me for not having my invention ready, and I was frustrated that I hadn't made one all semester. I couldn't think of a good idea for one. But now I'm in serious trouble. It's just a matter of time before I get caught, and then I'll get expelled."

I didn't say anything for a minute.

"I get why you did it," I said finally.

"You do?" Now Sunny was the one who looked surprised.

I should've felt happy that she wasn't the queen bee I thought she was; after all, this was Sunny, the one who got me in detention in the first place . . . but instead I just felt bad for her. "I'm not the popular kid you think I am," I said.

"Yeah, right—everyone's friends with you. You're even friends with the Sweet brothers!"

"I experienced the exact same thing as you. Out of the

blue this fall, everyone stopped worshipping me and Drew. The only reason kids in my grade were sorta friends with me was because I was friends with the Sweet brothers, and the only reason the twins liked me was because they thought I was a screw-up because I got detention, not like you. And they don't even like me anymore," I said.

"What about all those other kids you're friends with?" she asked.

I explained my side of the story, and afterward we sat there in a circle for a few minutes, not saying anything. It felt good to admit the truth to her, since she was the only person on the planet besides Drew who could possibly understand.

"You're kinda nuts, huh?" she said.

"Let's not forget that you have a closet full of other people's stuff," I pointed out.

Sunny frowned.

"So we're both fakes," she said, and I nodded. "I'm in big trouble, Peter. I need your help. Will you help me?"

It was the first time she'd ever needed my help for anything, and I felt shocked. "Of course," I said, and I was surprised at how fast I'd come to that conclusion. Sunny was surprised, too.

"Really?" she asked, eyeing me suspiciously.

"Don't you remember what Dad always says?" I asked. She shook her head, and I grinned. "Blood is thicker than water."

thirty

"WE'RE GOING TO HAVE TO RETURN the items," I said.

"But then I'll get busted," Sunny replied.

"Not if we do it anonymously, and make it so students think they just misplaced the stuff in their lockers. You know, like Dad's bike reflector."

"How do we do that?"

"We're going to need Drew's help. I don't think as well without him."

I went into my bedroom and called him up, and five minutes later he was in Sunny's bedroom. "Where's the monkey you found?" he asked.

"There is no monkey. I just needed you to come over," I admitted.

"I can't believe you'd say that."

"I can't believe you'd believe I'd found a monkey."

"Why'd you say there was a monkey?" Drew asked. "You know I would have come over, anyway."

I sighed. "I kinda lie a lot, if you haven't noticed."

"I've been meaning to talk to you about that, actually. It's really not a good—"

"You guys are idiots," Sunny said, and she whipped open the closet. Drew's eyes widened.

"You're the thief?" he asked, and she nodded. "But why would you steal from everybody?"

Sunny told Drew her story, and when she was done, he sat there on the ground for a minute, taking it all in. Finally he asked, "So how do we return everything?"

"One item at a time," I said, turning to my sister. "We use our strengths to our advantage to solve this mess. The way I see it, Drew and I are experts at scoping out danger, and another advantage we have is that nobody suspects you to be the thief, so you'll be the one to actually return the items while me and Drew look out for you. If we work together, we can return all the items without getting caught. Then it'll be as if the thief never existed. People will have no choice but to think they simply misplaced their stuff."

We spent an hour identifying where everyone's lockers were and their class schedules, and then sorted through the stolen items, putting the owner's names on Post-it notes so we'd know who each item belonged to.

"Let's make a promise," Sunny said at one point. "If we can somehow get out of this mess, then from now on we stop framing people into detention, stop stealing stuff, and start over from scratch."

The three of us shook on it.

"I didn't realize so many students had scarves," Drew said, going through the stolen items in the closet.

"That's because I stole them all," Sunny explained.

"That's funny!" Drew said. "I can see where Peter gets his humor."

"I'm not his mother, you moron," she snapped.

"I can see where he gets his temper, too," Drew added.

The next day we started returning the stolen items. Drew and I stood guard on opposite ends of the lockers, keeping an eye out for the student whose item Sunny was secretly returning. If they showed up, Drew and I would distract them. The first item we returned was Sally's horseshoe key chain. She was with her equestrian buddies next to her open locker after first period, so I looked out the window and shouted, "Hey, there's a wild horse in the parking lot!"

Sally and her friends rushed over to see. In the reflection of the window I saw Sunny slip the horseshoe key chain into Sally's locker. Drew coughed behind me, to let me know the mission was completed.

"Where is it?" Sally asked me.

I squinted out the window.

"Oh, woops, I guess it's just a motorcycle," I said.

She groaned.

"You need glasses, Peter," she said.

I held my arms out as if I was blind.

"Whoever said that, thank you, thank you for that tip, that helps," I shouted, then intentionally bumped my nose into the window, trying to leave. It hurt.

Drew wasn't as good at improvising when the student was around. Sunny waited near Carson's locker as he took out his science textbook, and Drew just copied my move and looked out the window and shouted, "Hey, there's a gigantic scientific calculator out in the parking lot!"

But Carson bought it, and he rushed over to the window. When Sunny was done returning his calculator, I coughed.

"Oh, false alarm," Drew said, frowning. "It's just a fire hydrant."

"You're insane," Carson said.

And that's how we did it. The first day we returned a dozen items and didn't once come close to getting busted. The next day we returned ten more. It took three days to return most of the items. There were a bunch of scarves and sweaters whose owners Sunny couldn't remember, but more importantly, there was only one major item left to return.

Ms. Schoonmaker's espresso machine.

thirty-one

IN DETENTION ON FRIDAY NOBODY talked to me. I sat by myself in the front row while Donnie did homework, the Sweet brothers worked on their mazes by themselves, and Sally and Trent passed notes to each other even though Mr. Tinsley couldn't hear anyone talking with his headphones on. Finally they realized that they didn't have to pass notes and talked loudly about what they were going to be for the Halloween pageant on Monday. The pageant is this annual tradition where the students wear costumes all day. Every year for no good reason they schedule it to take place a few days *after* Halloween's already passed, which kinda bums everyone out. Schools always schedule fun events after the holidays they're attached to on purpose, because they don't want students to be too spazzy or else riots could break out at assemblies and stuff. Sally was going to dress up as a unicorn, which I could've predicted. Trent was going to be one of the Boston Celtics just so he could have an excuse to dribble his basketball in the halls between periods for once. Halloween's usually my favorite holiday, but all I could think about was figuring out a way to sneak the espresso machine back into the teachers' lounge.

I closed my eyes and pictured the teachers' lounge. For the first time I pictured the one time I'd been inside it, when I'd asked Ms. Schoonmaker to get me out of detention. You could see the soccer field out the windows. There was an emergency exit right in the teachers' lounge, and I figured if we could cause some sort of distraction outside, surely all the teachers would rush out to try to catch us, and then Drew and I could use our land-skiing skills to sneak inside without anyone noticing, while Sunny returned the espresso machine!

"What are you smiling about?" Sally asked me.

"I don't know. Hey, is that your key chain? I thought it got stolen," I said, and Sally blushed. "And to think you accused me of being the thief."

She didn't say anything.

After detention I met up with Sunny and Drew in Corbett Canyon and pitched my idea. "It's not bad," Sunny said carefully. "But it's risky."

"Everyone's going to be wearing costumes all day, so we could wear Halloween masks so teachers won't be able to identify us," Drew suggested.

"I didn't even think of that," I admitted.

He drew an imaginary box with his fingers, and I nodded.

"This feels crazy, but it just might work," Sunny said.

"But will the teachers really rush out if we're outside?" I asked, starting to doubt my plan.

"We need something bigger, a reason for them to come out," Sunny said.

Drew raised his hand.

"You don't have to raise your hand," I explained. "It's just the three of us."

"I know what we can use to get them to come out," he said, bursting with pride. He went over to the safe and opened it up, pulling out his recorder/modified rocket launcher. "Me and Pete can have a bottle-rockets war!"

"Okay, so once all the teachers come out to get you two, I'll rush in and drop off the espresso machine," Sunny said, and we nodded. "The back door to the gym is always open, so you guys can sneak back in that way."

"This is going to work," Drew said.

"It has to," I said, looking at Sunny.

We went to the pawnshop to buy Halloween masks. We got six of them, and the pawnshop owner was real friendly to us, because we were by far his best customers at this point.

"We're going to have to train for this mission," Drew said as we all biked back home. "I haven't land-skied in over a month."

"What's land-skiing?" Sunny asked.

We took her over to the top of the big hill behind the soccer field at school. We stashed Sunny's duffel bag (which contained the remaining stolen items and the fireworks) under a tree at the edge of the soccer field for Monday.

"For this first run, just stay up here and watch what we do," Drew warned her. "Just to get a feel for how to do it."

She nodded.

"It's this way of moving faster than running down a hill," I explained. "You run, but with all the pine needles it's impossible not to slip and fall, so with land-skiing you launch yourself in the direction you want to turn, as if you're skiing moguls."

"I want to try," she said.

"It's too dangerous, and we're trained professionals," Drew said. "It's better if you just watch us first."

She rolled her eyes.

"Okay, on the count of three, first one down wins," I said to Drew, and he nodded. "One, two—hey, what's that behind you, Drew?—THREE!"

I took off a second before him. I nearly lost it in a patch of pine needles and did this cool move by accident where I half slid around a thick oak tree and kinda pulled myself back to the left by grabbing a branch and swinging myself back over. Drew caught up to me and we were side by side, barreling down the hill, when suddenly a shape passed between us. It was Sunny! She expertly weaved her way between branches and cut between trees, ducking under a big branch and sliding the last twenty feet at the bottom. Drew skidded to a stop next to her, and I ended up third.

"You're a natural," I said, feeling both impressed and deeply disappointed.

"I thought you were going to be terrible at first," Drew added. "How are you so good at this?"

Sunny looked cocky, but for once, it didn't infuriate me.

"This plan's definitely going to work," Drew said. "Right, Peter?"

"We can circle back from here, undetected, through the woods to the back entrance, and by sixth period Monday, Sunny will be in the clear," I said.

"Thanks, guys," Sunny said, and she looked like she meant it.

We climbed back up to the top to have an official race, because Sunny wanted to do it again. At the count of three we took off, and Sunny took the early lead. I managed to catch up to her, while Drew fell behind. Right before we reached the bottom, I took the lead and won the race! I looked over at Sunny. "Thanks," I said.

"You beat me fair and square, so there's nothing to thank me for," she said, but she was still smiling. Then her face changed. "Where's Drew?"

We looked behind us up the hill but couldn't see him at all. From the bottom of the hill the trees blocked the view—that's how steep it was. A couple of seconds later we heard him shouting, "Help me!"

My gut reaction was to run in the opposite direction, because it clearly sounded like Drew was either being attacked by a mountain lion or being held hostage by an escaped criminal, but since Drew was my best and only friend, I couldn't just ditch him, even though my life might be in danger. I cautiously edged forward a few feet and called out to him.

"What exactly do you mean by 'Help me?'" I shouted up the hill. "Are you with anyone or anything at the moment that could harm us as well?"

"Please, Peter, I'm hurt real bad!" Drew was crying loudly, but my mind was now picturing all kinds of terrible things in the woods (I'd added ghosts to my list of possible reasons why Drew was in pain). His cries echoed throughout the forest and it sounded to me like creepy laughter.

"Listen, I totally want to help you, Drew," I shouted. "But first I need to know if you're alone right now. Please work with me on this!"

There was no response at first. I craned my neck out from behind the safe cover of a big tree and for a second I swore I could make out the sound of chewing.

"I'm so cold," he finally cried out again, his voice noticeably weaker.

"You're not answering my question!" I shouted.

Sunny rolled her eyes at me.

"We have to help him," Sunny said, and started racing up the hill, while I frantically searched for a strong stick for protection. She turned back and glared at me. "Come on, Peter!"

We found Drew laid out on the ground near the top.

"What happened?" I asked.

"I twisted my ankle," he said, moaning. "Am I going to lose my leg?"

"Here, let me see," Sunny said. "Tell me if this hurts."

She barely touched his ankle with her pinky and he yowled in pain.

"Looks like you sprained your ankle. Do you think you can walk with our help?"

We helped him up, and then we had to ditch our bikes in the woods in order to hold him up on both sides all the way back home. It took nearly thirty minutes, and by then it was dinnertime.

"Ice it all weekend, okay?" Sunny said.

He nodded.

"What if his ankle's not better by Monday?" I asked her. "How will he be able to land-ski if he's on crutches or in a wheelchair?"

"I thought you guys said I wasn't going to lose my leg!" Drew whimpered.

"The plans have changed. Drew's going to have to return the espresso machine himself," Sunny said, staring at me. "I'm going to have to land-ski with you."

thirty-two

SUNNY GOT DROPPED OFF AT school early by Dad for band practice on Monday. The plan was that she'd meet me and Drew right before lunch by the gym. Drew and I walked to school together, and it took twice as long as usual because Drew was using one crutch for support. The rest of the morning passed by just as slowly. I felt like I was physically in pain, itching to get the mission over with. The bell for lunch rang, and Drew and Sunny and I met, as planned, over by the gym.

"Are you ready?" I asked Drew. "I mean, can you walk okay?"

"I'll be fine. I'm going to get in position."

Sunny handed him the bag with the espresso machine in it.

"It's really heavy," Drew said.

"Just make sure you don't go in if any teachers are in there. Look through the door window, and when you see them all rushing outside, you have maybe twenty seconds to safely do it. Don't mess around, put it on the counter by the sink, don't even plug it back in, and then get out of there, okay?" Sunny asked.

He nodded.

"I'm on it."

"This is going to work!" I said, and me and Drew high-fived.

"No celebrating until it's over," Sunny warned us. "Why do you always do that?"

"We don't often end up succeeding, so this way we still get to celebrate," I explained.

"That's really sad," she replied.

"Maybe you should try it—it might help you calm down about having to win everything all the time," Drew suggested.

She rolled her eyes.

"Come on, let's get this over with," she said.

Sunny and I made sure the gym teacher wasn't around before sneaking out the exit and booking it for the woods across the parking lot. We made it without being seen, and then we ran through the woods toward the hill. Our shoes got really dirty because the woods were muddy. We climbed up the hill and snuck over to the edge of the soccer field. Usually the sun glares off the windows of the school and you can't see inside, but it was cloudy out, and I could make out the shapes of heads moving around in the teachers' lounge. We pulled out the remaining stolen items and placed them on a dry patch of grass. I couldn't believe the stuff Sunny had stolen. In addition to the scarves, there was a wool sweater with holes in it, plastic hairclips, and a strange art project that looked like a tree with cotton balls for leaves. "What's that?" I asked.

"I don't know. I saw it in art class and grabbed it."

"You're crazy."

She shrugged her shoulders.

We had a bunch of bottle rockets, but Drew had come up with a good idea and added a Roman candle to really get the teachers' attention. It's this big stick that shoots colored fireballs out one end.

It was time. I gulped. I remembered that the reason me and Drew had all these fireworks in the first place was because back on the Fourth of July we'd been too scared to light them! I took a deep breath and managed with shaky hands to light the wick.

"Put your mask on," she said.

"Just don't stand right behind me, in case I'm not holding

the right end," I told her. The wick fizzled and it reached the inside of the Roman candle and then it . . . stopped.

"Oh no," I cried. "Is it a dud?"

"Tell me you brought another—," she started saying when the first fireball shot out.

It was amazing. A bright red ball of flame shot out, maybe fifty feet in the air! There was a slight kick, and it felt like I was shooting a real laser gun.

"I wish my hands could do this on their own," I said.

A second ball shot out a couple seconds later, this time bright green.

"Do you think they'll see this? It's daytime," Sunny asked.

I hadn't considered this fact.

"Who cares, this is so cool!" I said.

"Let me try," Sunny said, reaching for the Roman candle.

"Careful, it's not a toy!" I shouted.

"But it's halfway done, I want to feel what it's like, I never do stuff like this," she said. I let her take it, but she got scared and let go, and the Roman candle fell to the ground.

Uh-oh.

"Hit the deck, it's out of control!" I shouted, and we ran in circles trying to dodge the next ball. It shot out and nearly smacked Sunny in the chest.

"Grab it!" she shouted.

"You grab it," I replied. "You said you wanted to hold it!"

Suddenly three balls shot out one after another, all bright red, and unfortunately at this moment there was a pretty strong crosswind (we were in the middle of an open soccer field, after all). The Roman candle swiveled, shooting the last fireball directly at the pile, hitting the journals and scarves and the sweater and the cotton-ball tree thing. Almost immediately the duffel bag and the pile of stolen items caught fire. We gaped at each other for a moment.

"Well, that can't be good," she said.

"Put it out!" I snapped, and I tried to step on the scarf, but the fire was spreading quickly. "Why'd you have to steal so many cotton scarves?"

"Look, they see the smoke!" Sunny said.

Black smoke (some plastic hairclips had started melting) curled up from the top of the pile, and the door to the teachers' lounge opened and three teachers charged out. "What are you doing up there?" I could barely hear one of the teachers shout up at us.

"Let's bolt!" I said, and me and Sunny took off for the woods.

We land-skied down the hill, faster than I'd ever land-skied before, and as we tore down the hill I thought—aside from the pile of stolen items being engulfed in flames—our plan was actually going pretty smoothly. There I was, land-skiing down the hill with Sunny, of all people, and I had to admit that it was . . . fun. I looked over at her and I could tell she was thinking the same thing.

We used the woods as cover and made it to the back entrance without being seen, where we ditched the masks and put on the other ones we'd had in our back pockets. The only hitch in our plan was that the metal door was locked. "I thought you said the back door was always unlocked?" I said, gasping for breath.

"I guess I was wrong," she admitted. "We really could have planned this better."

"Maybe you're not the smart one," I replied.

The door opened. It was Mr. Tinsley.

"You two shouldn't be out here," he said. "Why are your shoes covered in mud?"

"Um, I thought I saw a . . . horse . . . calculator, out in the parking lot," I said lamely. I was suddenly worse than Drew at making up excuses on the fly.

"Horse calculator?" Mr. Tinsley said. "What the heck are you talking about?"

"Um, yeah, it's for horses, so it has these huge, hoof-shaped buttons, and—"

"Stop it, Peter," Sunny said. "It's too late."

"Tell your story to the principal," he said, and yanked us inside.

As we were going in, I glanced over at the soccer field.

The pile was still smoking.

"Let's just hope Drew got his end of the job done," I whispered to Sunny.

The secretary said that Principal Curtis was checking on something in the academic wing, so we waited in the orange puffy chairs outside his office. For five minutes we just sat there, me and Sunny, not saying anything. We weren't mad at each other, there just wasn't anything to say at that moment. Finally Mr. Tinsley and Principal Curtis showed up, and they both looked really mad.

"Here they are. I'm not surprised about Peter, since he's in detention all the time. But you, Sunny?" Mr. Tinsley looked at the principal.

"You two are in a heap of trouble," Principal Curtis said. "Setting fireworks off? Starting a fire on school property? What on earth were you two thinking?"

The principal stared at me, then at Sunny, then back at me. I wanted to just say "I don't know" like I always do with adults, but he looked like he was ready to bite my head off, so I said, "It's a long story."

"I'm all ears," he replied.

"Well, you see, this particular story has to do with a calculator, and, um, a horse—"

"Will you quit it with the horse calculator?" Sunny

shouted, and Mr. Tinsley was about to say something when the door burst open a second time, and Ms. Schoonmaker dragged Drew into the office by his shirt collar. He was hopping on his one good leg just to keep up with her, but she didn't seem to notice.

"We just caught Drew trying to return my espresso machine," she said. "He's the one who stole it last Tuesday."

"Drew Newmark? You're the thief? But you're so quiet," the principal said. He rubbed his temples. "Okay, I'm going to have a word with Drew, while you two wait here. I'll deal with you afterward."

Drew hobbled toward the principal's office.

"Wait," Sunny said, standing up.

Everyone looked at her.

"Drew, and Peter for that matter, were only trying to help me out. I stole the espresso maker," she said, her face bright red.

"Sunny—," I started, but she cut me off.

"These two shouldn't get in trouble. This is all my fault," she went on.

"Why would you steal my espresso maker?" Ms. Schoon-maker asked.

Sunny didn't say anything. She looked down at her shoes.

"Okay, now you two have to wait outside." Principal Cur-tis pointed at me and Drew. "I guess I now have to talk to

Sunny about this mess."

He patted his forehead with a balled-up napkin. This was seriously stressing him out. Suddenly I had an idea.

"Ms. Schoonmaker," I said, "Sunny only borrowed it because she was trying to get her invention done on time."

"What are you talking about?" she asked.

"She told me all about her invention. It's a home-security system called Mr. Home Security. The espresso machine is hooked up to the alarm system, so when the alarm gets tripped in the middle of the night, instead of an alarm going off, the espresso machine goes off in your bedroom, and you just lock the door and drink espresso while you wait for the police to arrive. That way you don't wake up all panicked and run the risk of having a heart attack. Instead of the blaring alarm, the amazing, delicious smell of espresso wakes you up, instead."

"Is that true, you stole it for the inventors' fair?" Ms. Schoonmaker asked her.

She looked at me, and I nodded with my eyes, and— proof that we were no longer mortal enemies—she totally understood what my eyes were saying.

"Yes, but I couldn't figure out how to make it work, originally I was going to use my parents' coffee machine, but I broke it trying to make the prototype, and then I was going to make it last Friday at school. . . ." Her voice trailed off.

"Well, I guess we'll have to take that into consideration," Ms. Schoonmaker said. "But that doesn't excuse stealing in the first place You should have talked to me, first. I might have been able to help."

"Is it really only Monday? Okay, you two boys better wait out here," the principal said, and then he closed the door to his office. Before the door shut, Sunny made eye contact with me.

At the very last second, she winked.

thirty-three

SUNNY ENDED UP GETTING DETENTION for the rest of the semester for stealing the espresso maker, while Drew also got detention for his involvement in the caper. I got an extra month added onto the detentions I'd already had left over, so for me it was like nothing changed. Oh, and Sally won the Halloween pageant, for being such a realistic-looking unicorn. And that's pretty much it. Almost. But I didn't tell any of this to Mom and Dad tonight, because, like I said at the beginning, there's no point to telling your parents the truth. They wouldn't understand it, which is why Sunny and I both played dumb when they tried to get answers out of us. Stealing, framing people, lying, setting massive fires on school property . . . they'd never be able to see things from our perspective, and they certainly would never believe that this afternoon's detention was actually a *good* thing, but it was.

I showed up late at room 12 this afternoon and was surprised to find that I was the only one there. The room seemed so cold and uninviting compared to back when I was framing students into detention. Mr. Tinsley showed up and rolled his eyes at me before sitting down at the front desk to grade some theme papers.

The door opened again a moment later, and it was Drew! It felt good to finally see my best buddy in detention with me, for once. He sat down next to me and immediately put his head down on his desk. "Why are you resting your head on the desk like that?" I asked.

"I've never been here before," he said. "Aren't we supposed to put our heads on the desks and be quiet the entire time?"

"We're not in fifth grade anymore," I explained. "Just sit normally, and we can even talk softly. Mr. Tinsley blasts his classical music the whole time, we just can't shout or else he'll yell at us."

"Really?"

"And we can draw, and play notebook games and stuff," I added.

"That doesn't sound all that bad, actually," he said, opening up his book bag. He looked around the otherwise empty room. "Looks like we have the place to ourselves."

Drew took out a pen and started intensely coloring in a page of his notebook so it was all blue (Drew's not that great a student, either) while I stared out the window, thinking about everything that had happened this fall.

Once upon a time, Drew and I were the kings of elementary school, and then when we got to Fenwick Middle we were suddenly considered losers, and so we did what we did to try to change things, and nothing worked, and we even broke up temporarily, and that was before things got really out of hand, but in the end we ended up right back where we started, losers at Fenwick Middle, but this time it didn't feel so bad.

In fact, maybe it even felt a little bit right.

The Sweet brothers showed up next, and Drew stiffened, but Hugh nodded wearily at both of us. "Hey, it's Street Magic and his assistant," he said, shaking his head. "You guys are psychos."

"I guess you were right about that detention theory," he whispered to me.

"I told you," I replied, before turning to Hugh. "Where's Trent and the rest of the gang?"

"Nobody else has been in here for days," he replied sadly. "I guess they weren't lifers like us."

Sunny showed up a moment later and sat down next to

us. She looked nervous.

"I can't believe you stole the espresso machine from the teachers' lounge," Hugh said. "Even I would never do something that crazy."

"Crazy runs in the family," I said, grinning at Sunny, but she was too stunned that the Sweet brothers didn't hate her to notice.

Even though I hated unicorns at this point, I started drawing one just because I now had at least thirty pictures of them in my notebooks, which I figured qualified as a decent-sized collection, but a moment later Sunny took my pencil away from me. "What do you think you're doing?" I asked.

"You're flunking out of sixth grade, remember?" she said. "I owe you one, so I'm going to help tutor you during detention so you pass your classes this semester. Take out your math homework."

"How about we brainstorm inventions together instead?" I suggested. "Have I ever told you about my mini cats idea?"

Drew rolled his eyes and Sunny wouldn't budge.

"Math first," Sunny said, crossing her arms.

Even though it was really nice of her to want to pay me back for helping her out, I hated doing homework. I mean, I'd never done it before, so technically I didn't know if I really hated it, but I had a good feeling that I would if I tried. Sunny stared at me until I sighed and took out my math folder.

"Try the first problem," she said. "Do you understand how to do it?"

I shook my head.

"What exactly do you not understand?" she asked. "Now's the time to ask. I need to know exactly how much you know if you want me to help you."

"Okay," I said, squinting at the page as if I'd never even seen this stuff before. "Well, for one thing, why's there a line between these two numbers?"

"Are you serious?" she asked, and I nodded. "That's called a fraction."

"I've heard of that!" I said.

I kept a straight face, and she gaped at me. At first it felt good to trick her, but then I felt insulted that she actually believed I didn't even know what a fraction was.

"You really don't think that highly of me, do you?" I said.

"Oh, brother."

Brother.

"Do you realize that might be the first time you've ever called me your brother in public?" I asked her.

"You know that's not how I meant it!"

"Close enough," I said.

"You are so weird."

After Sunny explained the basics, I started working on the first problem. I have to admit it felt really good to actually have a clue what I was doing, for once. Out of the corner of my eye I saw my sister gazing around the room.

"So this is detention, huh?" she finally asked me. "It's not so bad . . . kinda like our very own little club!"

I looked over at Drew—he was smiling at me. I turned back to Sunny.

"Something like that," I told her.

Acknowledgments

Words can't express the level of gratitude I feel for my editor, Donna Bray, but let's give it a go. . . . Punctual? Nice phone-voiced? Better than adequate? I'm also indebted to her cheerful underlings, Ruta Rimas and Jordan Brown, and I'd like to thank Alessandra Balzer and everyone else over at Balzer Plus Bray. And I wouldn't even be working with them if it weren't for Steve Malk. Lastly, I'd like to thank my friends and family, for being there for me when other peoples' friends and families weren't.